A FATHER THIS CHRISTMAS?

BY
LOUISA HEATON

Published in Great Britain 2015
by Mills & Boon, an imprint of Harlequin (UK) Limited,
Eton House, 18-24 Paradise Road, Richmond, Surrey, TW9 1SR

© 2015 Louisa Heaton

ISBN: 978-0-263-24744-2

Harlequin (UK) Limited's policy is to use papers that are natural,
renewable and recyclable products and made from wood grown in
sustainable forests. The logging and manufacturing processes conform
to the legal environmental regulations of the country of origin.

Printed and bound in Spain
by CPI, Barcelona

Eva swiveled in her seat and her eyes fell upon the one man she'd thought she'd never, *ever* see again.

Jacob Dolan. The doctor who'd slept with her four years ago and then run off to Africa. The doctor who'd got her pregnant and then disappeared without leaving a trace!

Why did he have to look so good?

This was her dream come true and her worst nightmare all rolled into one! Whilst once she had dreamed about what life might have been like for the pair of them if Jacob hadn't disappeared, she was now faced with the fact that he was back. And he would eventually need to be told about Seb.

'Eva?'

Chills trembled down her spine and she felt every single goosebump that prickled her skin.

'Jacob! Nice to see you again. It's been a long time.'

She held out her hand for him to shake, as one colleague would to another. He raised a quizzical eyebrow and shook it, smiling that kilowatt smile.

Oh, help…

Eva kept the smile plastered on her face, not knowing what else to do. She had momentous, life-changing news for this man. But how could she tell him?

Dear Reader,

I *love* Christmas. I love the countdown to the big day, the wishing and hoping for snow, the excitement of my children as they try to guess what they're getting… shaking and weighing up the presents under the tree. I love the food, the putting up of the decorations, and laughing at my husband as he tries—and struggles— to put up the Christmas lights each year.

As a child, I thought Christmas was special—but it meant even more when I watched my own children experience the season. For Eva and Jacob, Christmas means different things. For Eva it's a time that makes her feel even more separate from the family she was once with, and for Jacob it's a tragic reminder of a cruel event.

In this story we accompany them on their journey to find their own magic at Christmas—their own happy ending that they never believed could be possible. I hope you enjoy it.

Love and best wishes,

Louisa x

Louisa Heaton first started writing romance at school, and would take her stories in to show her friends, scrawled in a big red binder, with plenty of crossing out. She dreamt of romance herself, and after knowing her husband-to-be for only three weeks shocked her parents by accepting his marriage proposal. After four children—including a set of twins—and fifteen years of trying to get published, she finally received 'The Call'! Now she lives on Hayling Island, and when she's not busy as a First Responder creates her stories wandering along the wonderful Hampshire coastline with her two dogs, muttering to herself and scaring the locals.

Visit Louisa on twitter @louisaheaton, on Facebook Louisaheatonauthor or on her website: louisaheaton.com.

Books by Louisa Heaton

Mills & Boon Medical Romance

The Baby That Changed Her Life
His Perfect Bride?

Visit the Author Profile page
at millsandboon.co.uk for more titles.

To Mum and Dad,
who bought me a beautiful manual typewriter
one Christmas and released the story-writing bunny.

Lots of love, your loving daughter. xx

CHAPTER ONE

'QUICK, EVA, TAKE my pulse!'

Eva turned to her friend. What was wrong?

'What? Are you ill?'

She placed her fingers on Sarah's pulse point on her wrist and looked with concern at her friend as she counted beats. But Sarah wasn't looking at *her*—she was focussed on something or *someone* behind Eva, across the minors department, towards the entrance. She was seemingly fascinated, with a sparkle in her eyes and a slow smile creeping across her face as she looked someone up and down.

'Sex on a stick at one o'clock.'

'What?'

Why was she being ridiculous? Eva swivelled in her seat to see who was making Sarah act like that and her eyes fell upon the one man she'd thought she'd never, ever see again.

Jacob.

Dressed all in black, in what had to be tailored clothes, considering how well they fit, with his tousled dark hair and a five-o'clock shadow, a red-tubed stethoscope draped casually around his neck, he looked stunning.

Well dressed, powerful.

Virile.

More so than four years ago, if that were possible. Time had been overly generous to Jacob, bestowing upon him masculine maturity in a well-defined body that simply oozed sex appeal.

She'd begun to believe that she'd imagined this perfect man. That her one hot night with him that Christmas Eve four years ago had been a figment of her imagination. Despite the obvious, startling reminder that it *hadn't* been imaginary.

Their son.

Eva wanted the earth to swallow her up. Because then she wouldn't have to face him. Wouldn't have to explain to him that he was a father.

She could hardly believe that she had slept with a man she had only known for such a short time. Just because of something she'd felt when she'd looked at him. Taking him at face value—because, really, what else had she had to go on? He'd been in her arms, and they'd danced together in a slow, sultry melting of bodies... The way his hips had swayed, his groin had pressed against hers, the *feel* of him...

But now she was different. Stronger. She was no longer the young woman who had given her heart to a man who had only been a fantasy for just one night—a man she'd dreamed of after the fact.

Now she was more mature. A strong woman. A confident doctor. And there was no way she was going to let Jacob know how she was really feeling.

Terrified.

Still attracted...

I'm not! Just because it feels as if my heart is trying to leap from my chest...

She let go of Sarah's wrist and deliberately turned her back on him.

There was so much he needed to know! So much she needed to tell him. She'd searched for him. Tried to let him know about Seb. But it had been impossible! Would he understand?

Her mouth felt dry, as if it was full of sawdust, and she knew if she were to talk to him her tongue would just stumble over the words. She groaned as her stomach flipped and swirled like snowflakes in a snow globe.

'It's probably that new doctor Clarkson mentioned earlier.' She tried to sound as casual as she could. When Dr Clarkson, clinical lead of their A&E department, had mentioned they were getting a new doctor she'd initially been thrilled. Who *didn't* need an extra pair of hands in A&E after all? Even if it *was* just temporary cover for Christmas.

But he hadn't told her who was coming. Who the new doctor actually was.

Jacob Dolan.

The doctor who'd slept with her and then run off to Africa. The doctor who'd got her pregnant and then disappeared without leaving a trace!

Why did he have to look so good?

Sarah leaned forward to whisper to her, 'Oh, my goodness, I'd really love to find *him* in my Christmas stocking…' She licked her lips. 'How on earth are we going to get any work done with him hanging around? I'm going to be spending all my time wiping drool off my chin and hoping the cleaners have enough wet-floor signs to dot around me.'

Eva grimaced a smile, but went back to her paperwork. All she had to do was write these notes. Write these notes and then maybe get the earth to open up and swallow her or something. Once he realised she was here—once he realised that she was the woman who had slept with him four years ago…

She could grab her coat and go. She could say she was sick or something.

No...that wouldn't work. You only get a day off if you're dying—nothing less...

Their son.

She could tell Dr Clarkson it was something to do with Seb.

This was her dream come true and her worst nightmare all rolled into one! Whilst once she had dreamed about what life might have been like for the pair of them if Jacob hadn't disappeared, she was now faced with the fact that he was back. Here. In her department. And he would eventually need to be told about Seb.

She'd tried to tell him before.

I tried. I tried to track him down. But there was no trace! This isn't my fault! He can't hold me responsible for this!

She didn't have to think about him being here. About him actually being in her A&E department. Standing mere metres away, looking even more alluring than he had before, if that were possible.

She'd hoped her imagination had got it wrong. That her memories of him were impaired. That perhaps he'd *not* been that stunning. That perhaps he'd have more in common with Quasimodo, or a troll, or something hopeful like that.

'*Look* at him, Eva.' Sarah glanced at her friend and frowned. 'Eva? Why won't you look at him? Oh, he's coming over...' Sarah scraped back her chair and stood up.

Eva sucked in a deep, steadying breath and felt her heart pound against her rib cage. This couldn't be true! This couldn't be happening! Not now. She wasn't prepared for it. She'd dreamed about finding him and telling him about Seb for years, but now that the opportunity was upon her she was terrified.

'Eva?'

That voice.

Chills trembled down her spine and she felt every single goosebump that prickled her skin.

She could see Sarah glance at her in surprise that somehow Eva *knew* this man. No doubt there would be an interrogation later, and she'd want all the details, but Eva was mindful that not only was this her workplace but she was a professional—and what business was it of anybody but her?

She dredged up what she hoped was a pleasant smile from somewhere—hoping it didn't look like a ghastly rictus—and turned around, praying to any god that existed that she didn't flush like a menopausal woman or look as if she was going to pass out.

Those blue eyes...

'Jacob! Nice to see you again. It's been a long time.'

Was her voice as strangled as it sounded to her? She hoped not. She was determined to be as professional as she could be. Professional and *distanced*. She was at least grateful for the fact that her voice was actually working. She'd felt so trapped and cornered suddenly she was amazed her voice hadn't disappeared altogether, in a case of phobic aphasia.

She held out her hand for him to shake, as one colleague would to another. He raised a quizzical eyebrow and shook it, smiling that kilowatt smile.

Oh, help...

Eva kept the smile plastered on her face, not knowing what else to do. She had momentous, life-changing news for this man. But how could she tell him? Everyone knew she was a mother—it was bound to be mentioned to him at some point. All she needed was for someone to mention how old Seb was and Jacob would do a little maths, and then—

'How have you been?' he asked, smiling, looking her up and down. 'You look great.'

She lifted her chin and smiled. 'I've been fine. You?'

What had she expected? For him to say that his life had been awful without her? That after their one night he'd dreamed about her the way she had about him? *Hah!* Jacob Dolan had most likely coped absolutely fine without her!

'I've been good. I can't believe you actually work here.'

'Well, I do.' She struggled to think of something else to say. Something pleasant. Something...*neutral.* 'This is Sarah Chambers—another A&E colleague.'

She introduced her friend and Sarah practically melted over him, shaking his hand as if she'd never let go, as if his hand was somehow magically feeding her oxygen or something.

Eva rolled her eyes at her friend's blatant fawning, and when she could finally stand the overt flirting no longer she deliberately walked between them, so that their hand-shaking had to be broken off to allow her through.

'Let me introduce you to everyone.'

Jacob dropped into step beside her. 'Thanks. So...you're going to be my new boss?'

She shook her head. *No. Definitely not.* 'Dr Clarkson is clinical lead.'

'How long have you been here?'

'Since before I met you.' She grimaced at how easily she'd referred to when they'd met. Now he would be re-membering it, too.

She almost stopped walking. Couldn't believe she'd referred to it. Her stomach became a solid lump of cold ice. Her feet felt as if they were inside concrete boots and walking was like trying to wade through molasses.

How do I tell him?

'How was Africa?'

There. That was better. Turn the focus back onto him. It gave her time to breathe. Time to think. Time to formulate the answers she knew she'd have to provide.

'Hot. And dry. But amazing. Life-changing.'

There was something odd in his voice then, and she voluntarily turned to look at him, trying not to be pulled by the lure of those sexy blue eyes that had got her into so much trouble in the first place.

'It's been life-changing here, too. But it sounds like you might have a few stories to tell?'

She could tell *him* a few! About what had happened after he'd left. About the decisions she'd had to make. How she'd done everything alone—as always. But she couldn't right now. How could she? He'd only just got here. He'd only just arrived. Let the poor guy take his coat off before—

'I certainly do. We ought to catch up some time.'

He paused briefly, then reached out to catch her arm. Electricity crackled along her skin like a lightning strike.

'I'm glad you're here.'

His touch burned her skin and she stared at him in shock before pulling her arm free. Unable to stand his close contact, and the effect it was having on her breathing and pulse rate, she stepped farther away, putting a trolley between them and distracting herself by fiddling with the pressed bed sheets, pillowcases and yellow blankets piled upon it.

She picked up one or two and took great interest in folding and refolding them, giving herself time to recover from his touch. To cool down. For her heart rate to slow.

Time to think of something to say.

How *did* you tell a man that he was a father? Completely out of the blue?

By the way, you ought to know...you're a father.

No! She couldn't say it like that. It wasn't something

you could come straight out with. There had to be some sort of preamble. An introduction.

Jacob? You remember that night we spent together? Look, I know we used protection, but somehow it didn't work and...

Hmm... That didn't seem all that marvellous, either.

Jacob...there's no easy way to say this, so I'm just going to come straight out with it...you're a father.

'Let me show you around the department' was what she came up with.

That was easier. By being professional, by not actually looking at him, she could almost forget...almost pretend he was someone else. A junior, maybe. A complete stranger.

She led him around the Minors area and then into Majors, Resus, Triage, the waiting room, stockrooms, sluice and cubicles, talking nonstop about all kinds of things—hospital policy, staff rotas, tricks to know when dealing with the computer—anything and everything but the one thing she wished she *could* talk to him about but was afraid to tell him.

She was talking so he didn't have the chance to ask questions. And all the while aware of his proximity, his dark brooding outline, his expensive clothing, the feel of him near her once again.

She knew she was babbling. He was playing havoc with her senses. It was as if her body had been awoken by his presence. The way a flower reacted to the sun.

Her mind devilishly replayed a memory of his kiss. How his lips had felt upon hers. How they'd drifted ever so lightly across her skin, sending shivers of delicious delight through her body, arousing her nerve endings to touch in a way they had never been before, making her ache for more.

Eva could remember it all too well.

Every sizzling second of it.

Jacob had made her feel so *alive*! She'd had a long day at work that day, and when she'd made it to that party she'd felt exhausted—bereft of feeling. Yet in his arms she'd become energised, had tingled and yearned for his every touch, savouring every caress, consuming every desire and gasping her way through her ecstasy.

Feeling alive once again.

That one night had changed her entire life.

She shivered at the thought, those goosebumps rising again and her nipples hardening against her bra in expectancy. He was the only man who had ever made her feel that way. The only man she'd ever slept with since that night. The memory of him, the experience of him, had stopped her being intimate with any other. No one could measure up to his memory.

Not that there'd been anyone to challenge it, really.

Eva mumbled her way through the details of the filing system and how to operate the computer patient files, work through any glitches on the system, then asked him if he'd like to take on his first patient.

He cocked his head as he looked at her, trying to get her to make eye contact. 'You okay? I mean, I hope our having to work together isn't going to be uncomfortable?'

No, I'm not okay. You're back! You're back, and I had no warning. No time to prepare. And I have something momentous to tell you. And it will change your life. And I'm so aware of that and—

'I'm fine. It's…just been a difficult morning.'

He nodded in understanding. 'Anything I can help with?'

'No.'

He raised his eyebrow in such a perfect arch it was all she could do not to race into his arms there and then.

'Are you sure?'

How are you with kids? Do you even like children? Because I have some news for you...

Eva sighed and shook her head.

No, she wasn't sure.

She wasn't sure at all.

How to tell him that he was father to a beautiful, bright, funny, gorgeous three-year-old boy, who obsessed over lions and tigers and looked *exactly like him*?

She swallowed a lump in her throat as fear overturned her stomach. Nausea unsettled her. A close sweat beaded her brow as guilt and shame overflowed from the box where she normally kept all those feelings tightly locked away.

What was she to do?

Eva slammed a patient file down hard on the doctors' desk, the slap of cardboard on table echoing around the department, then sank heavily into a chair. Her fingertips punched into the keyboard as she began to write up some notes. She had no time. They were already running behind. Patients were filling up the waiting area and two were about to breach the four-hour limit.

Patients who had turned up because there were no district nurses to unblock catheters. Patients who were filling the corridors because there were no beds to put them in. Patients who were turning up just because they didn't want to be alone at home and they needed someone to talk to just a couple of weeks before Christmas.

The need to immerse herself in work and forget about the new doctor was overwhelming.

If she absorbed herself in work it wouldn't give her any time to think about *him*.

The guy who'd turned her neat little world around in just one night.

Even now she told herself she still didn't know what had happened that night. How had he managed to put her under his spell? She knew it had been a difficult and long day at work. She'd almost not gone to that stupid party. But it had been Christmas Eve, and she'd put herself down to work on Christmas Day, and the need to celebrate the season, despite not having any family of her own, had made her go. Just to have a drink or two with friends. Chill out for a moment.

And she'd done that. Had actually been enjoying herself for a brief time when she'd noticed him across the room.

Those eyes. Those piercing blue eyes. But she had noticed something in his gaze. A loss—a grief so deep it had called to her.

She'd recognised emotional pain. And, having been in a similar place herself, she'd hoped she could soothe him. No one had ever helped *her*. But maybe she could help him? Just for a moment, if nothing else.

Then, when he'd noticed her, something had happened. Something weird and dreamlike. As if the rest of the world had melted away and it had been just the two of them, standing in front of each other. Close. Almost touching. He'd said his name and then she'd been in his arms. Dancing with him. Swaying with him. Their bodies mirroring the other, blending together, matching the other.

Melting into one.

There'd been something magical that night.

And it seemed he was still magical now!

How involved would he want to be with his child? He might not even care! He might not want anything to do with them! Perhaps he'd be the type of guy who only paid child support. She wouldn't hate him for that. She'd be disappointed, but in fact she quite liked the idea that she wouldn't have to share Seb. She enjoyed it being just the two of them. It had always just been the two of them. She'd never had to share him.

Jacob could be in a relationship already with someone else. A man who looked the way he did? Of course he would be! A man like him wouldn't be single. If she'd ever entertained any grand idea that they would somehow end up together...

Her hand holding the pen trembled. She put it down for a moment and just sat for a second or two to pause and gather herself, to take in a deep breath and steady her jangled nerves. She could feel her heart slowing, could breathe more easily. Could act the professional doctor she believed herself to be.

Picking up her patient notes, she strode off to Minors.

Leo Rosetti had been brought in by his wife, Sonja. His knee hurt, and despite his taking painkillers at home nothing would touch it.

Eva entered the cubicle smiling, and closed the curtain behind her. 'Good morning, Mr Rosetti. I'm Eva, one of the doctors here in A&E. Can you tell me what's happened this morning to bring you in?'

There. That was better, she thought. Focus on the patients. Not on the fact that a certain someone had re-entered her life and turned it upside down and inside out.

'Well, Doctor, I've got this terrible pain here.' He leaned forward on the bed and rubbed at his left knee through his trousers. 'It's awful, I tell you. Really hurts.'

'And how long has it been like this?'

'Since the beginning of December now, and I really don't feel well in myself, either. It's not good for a person to live with pain day after day.'

No. It wasn't. Especially the emotional kind.

'He's diabetic, Doctor,' the wife interjected. 'And he's got osteoarthritis in both his knees. Had it for years. But he says this is different.'

Eva asked if he could roll up his trouser leg and she examined the grossly swollen knee. 'Are you on any meds, Mr Rosetti?'

'Leo, Doctor, please. I'm on metformin for the diabetes.'

She gave him a general check and then carried out a primary survey, asking questions about his general state of health, taking his BP and arranging for a full blood count and an X-ray, even though Leo said he hadn't knocked or damaged the knee as far as he knew.

'Will he be all right, Doctor? We're going away this weekend.'

'Oh, yes? Anywhere nice?'

'Africa—well, Kenya specifically. We're going on safari. Thought we'd do something different for Christmas, now that the kids have flown the nest.'

Africa. What *was* it with Africa?

She coloured as she thought of Jacob and what it had been like to see him again. That intense look in his eyes. Still with the power to make her go all weak at the knees as it once had.

Feeling guilty at having let her mind wander whilst she was with a patient, she smiled quickly. 'I'll be back in a moment to do the bloods.'

She pulled the curtain across and exhaled quietly and slowly, closing her eyes as she tried to gather her thoughts, her hand still clutching the curtain.

Seriously—what was going on here? Why was she allowing herself to get so worked up?

So Jacob was here? Big deal! He was just a guy. Just a…

I need to pull myself together!

This was not like her! She was normally an organised person. Efficient. She didn't get distracted at work! There was too much at stake to let personal feelings get in the way whilst she was there.

A distracted doctor was a dangerous doctor.

She hurried back to her seat to write up her notes, managing a weak smile as Sarah settled next to her.

'You okay?'

'Sure!' She tried to answer cheerily. 'Just...you know... busy.'

'Really? You seem a bit flushed about that new guy. Anything I can do?'

'Short of growing another pair of arms? Seriously, I could really do without having to babysit a new doctor—'

'So how do you know him?'

Her cheeks burned hot. 'I don't—not really. We only met once before.'

'Come on! He knew your name! You *know* him. How come?'

Eva stared hard at her friend, afraid to give the answer. Afraid to voice the thing that mattered the most to her in the whole world.

Because he's Seb's father.

She muttered something unintelligible and hurried away.

Her patient, Leo, had his bloods done and sent off, and also an X-ray that showed osteoarthritic changes and some mild widening in the joint space of his knee. The blood cultures wouldn't be available for three days, but his Hb levels were normal.

As the knee itself was hot and swollen, she felt it was wise to do a fine needle aspiration to draw off some of the fluid for testing. As she did so she noted that the fluid was quite cloudy, and she marked the tests to check for white blood cell count with differential, gram stain and culture.

She suspected a septic arthritis, and knew the joint would probably have to be drained until dry, as often as was necessary.

'It shouldn't affect your holiday as it's important you keep moving, Leo.'

Mr Rosetti and his wife smiled at each other, and she was about to leave them alone and send the aspirated fluid to Pathology, when Jacob pulled open the curtain and asked if he could have a quick word.

Excusing herself from her patient, she stepped outside of the cubicle with him, feeling her heart race once again. What did he want? Had he found out about Seb?

Her brain quickly tried to formulate an answer about that. 'Look, I meant to—'

'There's been a road accident. We've been phoned to let us know that a number of child casualties are coming our way.'

Children? Eva's heart sank. She could only hope that the children about to come into the department would have simple minor injuries.

They began a hurried walk to Resus. Eva's mind was focused firmly on the news. 'Any idea of the number of casualties?'

'Not at this stage. But it was a school minibus carrying a number of children across town. The police suspect they hit some black ice.'

Her heart thumped hard. She knew Seb's school had been attending a Christmas church service today.

'What age range?'

'We don't have any more details yet.'

It *couldn't* be Seb's school, Eva thought. Someone would have phoned her already.

'Has anyone let Paeds know?'

He nodded. 'I did. They're sending a team down as soon as they've got people to spare.'

'There's no one free *now*?'

What was she doing? She shouldn't raise her voice at him. It wasn't his fault, was it?

They burst through into Resus.

'What's the ETA?'

A nurse put down the phone. 'Seven minutes.'

'Let's get organised. Check equipment trolleys, monitors, sterile packs, gauze—everything and anything. We've an unknown number of paediatric casualties coming in and I want this to run smoothly. Let's prepare for crush injuries, possible fractures, whiplash and maybe burns. Have we ordered blood?'

Sarah and another doctor, Brandon, arrived in Resus.

'We're on it.'

She nodded at both of them. 'I'll lead team one—Sarah, you can be team two… Brandon three.'

'Where do you want me?' asked Jacob.

Ideally as far away from me as possible.

'Work with Brandon.'

'Okay.'

He wrapped a plastic apron around himself and grabbed for gloves before glancing at the clock, walking away to join Brandon.

She watched him go, knowing that at some point she was going to have to tell him the truth.

Just not now.

Six minutes to go.

Eva pulled on her own apron and donned gloves, her

heart pounding, her pulse thrumming like a well-oiled racing car.

Five minutes.

All eyes were on the clock.

Watching it tick down.

CHAPTER TWO

AMBULANCE SIRENS GREW louder and closer as the staff waited, tense and raring to go. These were the moments that Eva both loved and hated.

Loved because of the way Resus went quiet as they all waited, pensive, with adrenaline urging their muscles to get moving.

Hated because she never quite knew what horrors she might yet encounter.

Still the paediatric team had not arrived.

Outside, there was the sound of rumbling engines and then the distant beeping sound of a reversing vehicle. Hospital doors slid open as the first patient came in.

Eva spotted a small dark-haired child, wearing a neck brace and on a backboard, and heard the paramedic firing off details about the patient.

'This is Ariana, aged three. Ariana was restrained by a seat belt but endured a side impact of about thirty miles an hour. Head to toe: small abrasion on the forehead, complaining of neck pain, score of eight, bruising across the chest and middle, due to the seat belt, lower back and pelvis pain, which is secured with a splint, GCS of fifteen throughout, BP and pulse normal.'

Ariana? Didn't her son Seb know a girl in his nursery school called Ariana?

Eva tried not to panic. She had to focus on the little girl in her care. Surely the school would have rung her if anything had happened to Seb? Although her phone was turned off, of course, and in her locker. She'd run and check as soon as she got the chance. Ariana was her priority right now.

'Ariana? My name's Eva. I'm one of the doctors here and I'm going to look after you.'

The way you dealt with any patient was important, but when it came to dealing with children—children who didn't yet have their parents there to advocate for them— Eva felt it was doubly important. You *had* to let them know it was okay to be scared, but that they would be looked after very well and that the staff would do their utmost to get the child's parents there as quickly as possible.

Ariana looked terrified. She had a bad graze on her forehead, probably from smashed glass, and her eyes were wide and tearful. Her bottom lip was trembling and it was obvious she was trying not to cry.

Eva's heart went out to her. How terrifying it must be to be that small, alone and hurt, in a strange place that smelled funny and sounded funny, surrounded by strangers who all wanted to poke you and prod at you and stick you with needles, saying they'd make you feel better.

'We need to check you're okay, Ariana. What a pretty name! Now, I'm just going to use this—' she held up her stethoscope '—to listen to your chest. Is that all right?' Eva always made sure her paediatric patients understood what she was doing.

Ariana tried to nod, but her head's movement was restricted by the neck immobiliser. 'Ow! It hurts!'

'Which bit hurts, honey?'

'My neck.'

'Okay, I'll check that out for you in just a moment.'

Ariana's chest sounded clear, which was a good sign. However, neck pain was not. It could simply be whiplash, but with neck pain you never took a chance.

'We'll need to take a couple of special pictures. But don't you worry—they won't hurt. It's just a big camera.'

She looked up at the team she was working with, awaiting their feedback. One was checking the patient's airway, another was checking her breathing, another Ariana's circulation. One would get IV access for the admission of drugs or painkillers or blood, if it was needed. Each doctor or nurse was calling out a result or observation. They all worked as a highly efficient team so that patients were quickly and perfectly assessed as soon as they arrived in Resus.

Ariana was looking good at the moment. With the exception of the neck pain and the pelvic brace she was doing well, and she was responsive, which was very important. Her blood pressure was stable, so hopefully that meant no internal bleeding at all for them to worry about.

Behind her, Eva heard the Resus doors bang open once again as another patient arrived from the accident. She risked a quick glance to see who had come in. She knew Sarah or Brandon would take care of the new patient and she could focus all her attention on Ariana.

'Have the parents been called?'

One of the nurses replied, 'We believe the school are trying to contact parents now.'

'Good. Did you hear that, Ariana? We're going to find your mummy and daddy.'

She couldn't imagine what it must be like to get that call, being a mother herself. Luckily, so far, Seb hadn't been involved in anything serious like that. The only time she'd ever been woken by a phone call was when he'd gone for a sleepover at a friend's house and the mother had rung at about eleven o'clock at night to say that Seb couldn't get to sleep without his cuddly lion.

Nothing like this, thank goodness.

But having Ariana in front of her was making her doubtful. This sweet little girl looked familiar, and she felt *so sure* that Seb had a girl in his nursery class called Ariana…

If it *was* the same preschool as Seb… If he'd been hurt…

Her stomach did a crazy tumble.

She glanced across at the other teams. Sarah was busy assessing a patient and Brandon and Jacob were looking after their own little charge.

She turned back to Ariana, who was now holding her hand, and showed her the Wong-Baker FACES pain-rating scale—a series of cartoon faces that helped really young children scale their pain.

'Which one of these are you, Ariana? Zero? Which means no hurting? Or ten? Which means hurting the worst?'

She watched as Ariana looked at all the little cartoon faces and pointed at four—'Hurts A Little More'.

Good—the painkillers were taking effect. Hopefully that four would drop. Earlier, the paramedic had said her pain score was eight, so it was better, even if it wasn't perfect.

Eva continued to hold Ariana's hand. It was a soothing thing to do whilst they waited for their turn at CT and X-ray. If it had been Seb trapped in a hospital bed she would hope that the doctor caring for him would do the same thing, too, until she arrived.

Ariana's CT scan was clear. The computer tomography scan showed internal slices through the body, so that breaks or bleeds could be seen much more clearly. Her pelvis was fine, as was her neck. Eva decided that she'd wait until they got back to Resus before she took off the immobiliser from Ariana's neck and the brace from her pelvis.

As they wheeled her out of CT one of the nurses let Eva know that Ariana's parents were on their way.

When they arrived back in the department Eva made the decision to take Ariana to the cubicles. Minors was busy, as some of the lesser injured children from the minibus had filled it up, and they still had a waiting room full of patients who hadn't been involved but had come in with various ailments or injuries.

'We'll wait in here for Mummy and Daddy. This is much less scary than where we were before, isn't it?' She smiled at her patient.

Ariana was looking much happier now that the immobiliser and brace were off. She'd been a very lucky girl.

'Ariana...I know you were going on a trip with your nursery. Which nursery do you go to?'

Please don't say Pear Tree Pre-School!

'The one next to the big school.'

Pear Tree Pre-School was next to an infant school...

'What's your teacher's name?'

Seb's teacher was Miss Dale. She was a very pretty young woman, with the sweetest nature, and Eva secretly wondered how she managed to keep her perfect composure all day long when surrounded by thirty-odd preschoolers.

'Miss Dale.'

Oh, my God! Seb!

'Ariana, I just need to check on something. Stay here, honey.'

She yanked open the curtain and fled from the cubicle, flagging down a passing nurse to sit with Ariana before heading straight to the minors board, looking for her son's name.

Her eyes skim-read all the names until she saw it: Corday, Sebastian.

Please let him be all right!

She was about to rush off and find him when she did a double take, noticing the name of the doctor tending to him.

Jacob Dolan.

A sick chill had pervaded her body and her limbs felt numb and lifeless.

Jacob was with his son and he didn't even know it!

Seb was talking to his father and he had no clue!

She forced her limbs to move. Forced her heavy body to start making its way to the cubicle where her life would change drastically.

Cubicle number four.

What were they talking about? Seb couldn't be that injured if he was in Minors, but how bad was he? Was he sitting up in bed, chatting with his father? Was her secret out already?

No, not possible. Surely...?

Eva walked towards the cubicle with its closed curtain, a feeling of dread sitting low and heavy in her stomach. She could hear laughter inside, and Seb's gentle chuckling.

She was just about to pull the curtain back when she felt a hand on her arm.

Sarah and Brandon wanted to give feedback. One child had a small fracture of the wrist and severe bruising where the seat belt had crossed the body. Another had dislocated her shoulder, but it had been reduced and put into a sling. The teacher driving and all the other adults had got away with nothing more than whiplash and bruising.

'Nothing more severe? Thank goodness for that. They've been lucky, all of them.'

As Sarah and Brandon went back to their respective

charges Eva couldn't help but relax her shoulders, but she took a deep breath before she whipped back the curtain.

Seb was sitting up in bed, a broad smile on a face that was peppered with cuts. Jacob was seated on a stool next to him, about to glue a cut on his scalp.

'Mummy!' Seb saw her and lifted his arms for a cuddle.

Eva hurried over to him, waiting for the axe to fall, waiting for Jacob to do the maths and accuse her of being some heartless witch...

'Seb! Are you okay?'

Jacob held off with the glue, giving them a moment. 'Hello, Seb's mum.'

She chose not to look at Jacob, knowing that if she did her eyes would give her away. Instead, she rapidly checked her son over, her hands grasping at his limbs, feeling for hidden injury. Apart from the cut on his scalp, he didn't seem too bad.

She picked up his chart from the end of the bed and read through it. 'Nothing serious, thank goodness.'

Jacob was watching her. 'Just some minor cuts and scratches, thankfully. His head was banged against the side window, which has given him the small laceration that I was going to glue. He should be fine.'

'Does he need a head CT?'

'Dr Ranjit has checked him and said it wasn't necessary.'

Dr Ranjit was a paediatric neurologist, so she had to assume he was right. 'I see...'

'Seb and I were just talking about lions. Apparently they're his favourite animal.'

'He loves lions.'

Jacob tilted his head at her curt tone, looking at her curiously. Then he asked Seb to put his head back against the pillow so that he could administer the glue. 'Be brave, now—this might tingle a bit.'

Eva gripped her son's hand tightly, smiling brightly into his face to encourage him to be brave.

He looked *so* like Jacob! Couldn't Jacob see it? They both had the same almost black hair, slightly wavy. The same bright blue eyes…the same nose and mouth. It seemed that when genetics were being decided upon Mother Nature had decided to give Seb only his mother's skin tone—very pale and creamy, with hints of pink in his cheeks. Apart from that, he was the spitting image of his father.

And this was not how she'd wanted Jacob to find out. She'd wanted to be able to tell him somewhere peaceful and neutral—perhaps the hospital grounds in a secluded corner? To buy him a coffee and ask him if he had time for a chat, and then slowly drip feed the information about what had happened after he left.

Not like this. Not in front of her son!

Seb winced as the glue went onto the edges of his wound and Jacob pinched them together to help them adhere.

'You're doing great, honey.' Eva rubbed his hands in hers and wished she could take away the pain. The discomfort. Do what she could to make her son feel better.

'I didn't know you were a mother.'

She looked at Jacob quickly, and then away, guilt flooding her cheeks with heat. 'No, well…things change.'

'How old are you, Seb?' he asked, frowning.

'Three.' Seb smiled. 'It doesn't hurt now.'

Jacob nodded and let go, and the wound's edges stayed together. He pulled off his gloves and smiled. 'There you go. It doesn't need a plaster or anything. Just don't get it wet. Well done, Seb! You're very brave.'

Seb beamed with pleasure.

'Can I take him home now?' Eva started to gather her son's things. His backpack had been put on the end of his bed, and his jacket.

'He needs to stay here for an hour or two for observation. He *has* had a bump to the head.'

He was staring at her, his eyes full of questions.

He knows!

She had to get out of there! She did not want to have this conversation in front of Seb! She would *not* have this conversation in front of him. No. Not at all.

But he had to stay. For observation. Couldn't she observe him at home? She was an A&E doctor after all...

'May I have a word with you, Dr Corday?'

Oh, this is it. Here it comes...

'Sure. But...um...later, maybe? I need to arrange cover if I'm going home.'

'Could we talk *now*?'

She looked at Seb. Then back at Jacob.

'Let me get him sorted first.'

She rummaged in his backpack and found his reading book. She passed it to him.

'Have a read of your book, Seb. I'm just going to step outside the curtains and have a talk with Dr Dolan.'

Eva followed Jacob from the cubicle and went with him over to the quiet corner by the Christmas tree.

It looked beautiful this year. The team had really done themselves proud. For years they'd had a tired old fake tree that had been packed away each year in an old cardboard box, battered and unloved. But this year they had a real tree, beautifully decorated in gold and silver, with lots of pretend presents underneath.

Eva and Seb had been really looking forward to Christmas. This year it seemed Seb really understood what was going on, and what was happening, and the story of Santa

Claus had got him so excited! They'd already put their own tree up at home.

But Eva wasn't excited right now. She felt dread. And guilt. All those emotions she'd kept hidden away for years, since that first night with Jacob, neatly locked down, were now threatening to overwhelm her with their enormity.

She stood in front of Jacob like a naughty child before the headmaster. But then she thought about how he was guilty, too. About his part in all of this.

She squared her shoulders back and looked him in the eye. 'Yes?'

'You seem a little…distracted.'

She said nothing. Just stared at him. Waiting for the axe to fall.

'Seb's a great kid.'

'He is. The best.'

'You weren't a mother when we met.'

Her cheeks flamed. 'No.'

'But you are now. And he's three?'

'Yes.'

Jacob seemed to be mulling over his next words. Thinking about what he might say next. Whether she would rebut his words or accept them.

'He looks like me.'

Eva stared deeply into his bright blue eyes…eyes so much like Seb's. She couldn't—wouldn't—deny him the truth. He deserved that.

'Yes.'

Jacob's voice lowered. 'Is he mine, Eva?'

Of course he's yours! Surely it's clear to everyone?

She wanted to yell. She wanted to confirm it to him angrily. Rage at him for all he'd put her through after he left. But she didn't. She knew that could come later. Right now he just needed the plain facts.

'Yes. Seb's your son.'

He stood staring at her, his face incredulous.

The Christmas tree twinkled between them.

She couldn't help but notice how his broad shoulders narrowed down into a neat, flat waist. How his expensively tailored trousers moulded his shape, his long, muscular legs. He looked mouth-wateringly good. The years he'd spent in Africa had obviously been good to him. He was vital and in peak condition.

Years before, when they'd met at that party, there'd been only hints of the man he was to become. But even then he'd been delicious… Now the heavier muscle and perfectly toned body looked amazing on him…

She swallowed hard.

All she'd known about him that night was his name and that he was going to work for some charity. That he was a doctor, like her, and was going to Africa. But just because that was what he'd said, she hadn't been sure it was true. People lied. Especially at parties. To make themselves sound better or more interesting than they actually were.

Jacob. In *her* A&E. Standing there. As large as life. As gorgeous and as sexy as he'd ever been. A hundred times more so.

He was just staring back at her, his mouth slightly open, as if he'd had something he was about to say only it had never come out.

She couldn't just stand there! Waiting for the axe to fall. To see his reaction. Waiting for him to reject them.

So Eva turned and headed in the opposite direction—back through the curtains of the cubicle that held her son.

Their son.

If she just accepted right now that Jacob wasn't going to be sticking around—he was just a locum after all, here for the busy Christmas period—then it wouldn't hurt as badly.

She couldn't expect him to stay. She and Seb deserved to be loved 100 percent. Eva refused to accept anything less.

'Seb will be okay to go home soon. I'll have to take the rest of the day off. There's no one else to take him, and I can't get my neighbour Letty in—not after this.'

'The new doc can pick up the slack,' Sarah said.

'Jacob.' Her mouth and lips and tongue flowed over his name like a caress.

Eva turned to go and get Seb, then realised her coat and bag were in her locker on the other side of the department. She hurried to get them, flushing as she went past the double doors to Resus.

She had to be quick. Her fingers fumbled over the combination lock and her hands were shaking by the time she managed to open it.

She'd worried so much about how Jacob would react upon finding out he had a son that she hadn't given a thought as to how *Seb* might react if he found out! He didn't even know he *had* a father. Seb hadn't yet asked, and she'd been too afraid to broach the subject with her very young son, deciding to wait until he was older to tell him what little she knew about Jacob.

Eva hurried from the staff locker room and headed for the cubicles.

She wanted to go home *now*!

CHAPTER THREE

HE HAD A SON? A *son*!

That little boy. Seb. He'd just been *talking* to him, taking care of him, and he'd not once suspected that he was his son.

But why would he? Just because the boy had had the same hair as him and the same eye colour…that didn't mean he should have suspected at all…

Why the hell hadn't Eva told him about Seb? Why had she kept him a secret?

He couldn't bear that. Secrets were dangerous.

He had to talk to her. Find out more. Find out what had happened after he left.

Walking away from the Christmas tree, he headed back to the cubicles—only to find Eva there, putting on her coat and scarf.

'Where are you going?'

'Home. I can observe Seb there. I *am* qualified.'

'He needs to stay here.'

She looked at him. 'This is nothing to do with you. You don't have to pretend to care.'

'Seb is *everything* to do with me—and not just as his doctor. And I do care.'

Eva stared at him, and as he waited for her to say something Seb peeked at him over his book and smiled.

Jacob couldn't help but smile back. Seb was a cute little guy.

Then he looked back at Eva. 'You both need to stay. We need to talk.'

She shook her head. 'I'm not ready for this right now.'

'Tough. It's happening.'

He dared her to defy him. If she chose to walk away right now, then he had no idea what he would say. He'd probably have to chase her until she gave up and headed back to A&E. But thankfully he didn't have to do any of that.

Eva let out a big huff, and then removed her scarf and unbuttoned her coat. 'Fine.'

Jacob let out a breath and his shoulders sagged down. He hadn't realised how tense he'd been. He couldn't help but look at Seb now.

He looked tall for a three-year-old. Like himself, he supposed. He could remember his mum saying that he'd always been tall for his age. Then again, Eva wasn't short, either. But now, the more he looked at his son the more he could see himself in the little boy. Seb's eyes were the same shape and colour as his, he had the same wavy hair, the same shaped mouth…

It was like looking at a mini-me.

And he was *three* years old…

Three years that he had missed out on. Three years of important milestones—his first word, his first steps, his first tooth, his first Christmas!

I've missed everything. Birthdays and Christmases…

How had he not known about his own son? More important, why had Eva kept it from him? For three years! The last woman who had kept a secret from him had almost destroyed him.

Jacob called for one of the healthcare assistants to sit

with Seb. 'Don't let him out of your sight,' he said, then guided Eva into the staff room and slammed the door closed behind them.

Three years! I've had a son for three years and she never told me!

Fury and rage that he'd never thought it possible for one human being to contain filled his body, making it quake, and he had to grit his teeth to try to bring it under some form of control.

'What the *hell* have you done?'

She looked up at him, her eyes wide and defiant as a solitary tear dribbled down her face. Even crying she was beautiful, and he hated her for that. Why couldn't she look wretched? Why couldn't she look awful, as if she were suffering for the pain she'd caused him?

He recalled Michelle standing in front of him, crying, begging for his forgiveness...

'I've done nothing wrong.'

He looked at her, incredulous. 'Nothing *wrong*?'

'I'm raising a boy on my own and I'm doing a damned fine job, thank you very much!'

'Oh, I'm sure that you are—but what about me? Did you not think our son deserved a father?'

'Of course I did!'

A horrible thought occurred to him. 'Are you with someone else? Is another man raising my child?'

She shook her head. 'No.'

'Then, why didn't you find me and tell me?'

'I tried! Believe me, I tried! But I only had your name, and I knew you were going to work for a charity in Africa. I had no way to track you down.'

'Did you even try?'

She wiped the tear from her cheek. 'Do you know how

many charities do work in Africa? Do you know how much research that would have taken?'

'You could have asked my friends from the party! They would have known!'

'I did! They told me you were working with Change for Children, but when I contacted them, they told me you'd already left!'

He stared at her. It was true. He had worked for them, but only for a little while. And then he'd met that doctor working for a different charity and he'd gone with him, hoping to assist with an eye clinic…

Had he told anyone? Had he told anyone the specifics of where he was going next? He couldn't remember. Surely he must have said something? But even if he had, would she have been able to track him down? He'd still been running then. He would not have left a way for himself to be traced by his family…

Was all this *his* fault? If he'd only thought to leave a forwarding address… Only he hadn't, had he? Because he'd been trying to avoid his family tracking him down and sending him letters, bothering him with all their worry and their 'Are you all right?' and 'Are you coming home?'

He'd always assumed that when the time came he would be there for his children. As his father had been for him. He'd imagined what it might be like to hold his baby in his arms… And Eva had had his child, not found him to tell him about it, and his own son had been without him for three years. If he'd known he wouldn't have stayed in Africa for so long…or even gone there in the first place!

Words couldn't adequately describe how angry he felt right now.

And for it to be *Eva* who had done this to him. The woman who had sashayed into his life one night, blown his mind and made him feel more alive than he'd felt in a year! The woman who'd filled his dreams for many a night subsequently. The woman who'd made him regret leaving England. The woman he'd thought about coming back home for.

He'd never have expected that *she* would do this to him!

'So…what does Seb know about me?'

She folded her arms. 'Nothing yet. He's too young to have asked about his dad. I had planned, when the time came, to tell him that you were in Africa, with no means of communication.'

'Africa…'

He'd loved it there. It had been such an education for him—would have been for any doctor—to go from a high-tech medicalised hospital to work in a ramshackle, dusty building that barely had instruments, lights or monitoring equipment. Many a time he'd been so frustrated at the lack of equipment, at the numbers of people they'd lost because they didn't have adequate resources, that he'd decided to come home again and again, after every loss, but he never had.

If only I had…

Then he might have learned about Seb sooner. Learned about Eva. Could he forgive her? This was Eva—the woman he'd…

Jacob cleared his throat. 'I've lost so much time with him already. He needs to know who I am.'

She stood up instantly, her body blocking the door. 'You're not going in there to tell him right now.'

He raised an eyebrow. 'He needs to know.'

Eva nodded. 'Then, I'll tell him. At home. In his own space. Then maybe… I don't know…perhaps you could come round later? Get to know him? Next week, perhaps…'

'Give me your address. I'll be round tonight.'

'Tonight? I don't—'

'Tonight. I've already lost three years.'

She looked down at the ground. 'I need more time.'

Jacob stepped forward so that he faced her, his nose mere inches away from hers. 'You've already had three years. Tell him today. Or we both tell him tonight, when I come round. Your call.'

Eva backed away from the intense, angry stare of Jacob's eyes. She'd had no idea of how angry he'd be. Or, really, what type of man he was. She'd allowed herself to be seduced by a stranger that night. She only knew one side of him.

'I'll tell him. I was the one who kept it from him after all.'

The way she looked at him then, with those beautiful crystal blue eyes of hers—the palest of blue, like snow ice on the polar caps—he had a flashback to how those eyes had looked into his that night they'd spent together, and a smack of desire hit him hard and low in the groin.

How could he still desire her when she'd just driven him mad with anger?

'You know what hurts the most, Eva?'

She shook her head, her full, soft lips slightly apart, so he had to fight the urge to kiss her. It was as if there was a battle going on in his body. Half of him wanted to be furious with her; the other half wanted to take her to bed and make her gasp with delight.

'Not only did you keep Seb from *me*, you also kept Seb from my parents. Grandparents who would love him. Aunts and uncles who would adore him. Cousins who could be his friends. My family would *adore* Seb.'

'They still can...'

'But only because I came here.' He reached up and re-moved a wave of red hair from her cheek, then realised what he was doing and dropped it like a hot coal. 'How much longer would you have kept the secret if I'd gone elsewhere?'

She seemed nervous of his touch, her breath hitching in her lungs and then escaping when he let go of her hair. She was breathing heavily, and he felt empowered to know he had that control over her. That she still responded to his touch.

He'd never forgotten that one night...

'Jacob, I—'

'What's your address?'

Reluctantly, she told him.

He stepped past her and yanked open the locker room door.

'I'll be round at six.'

And then he left, leaving her alone.

Eva stood gasping like a landed fish after he'd left the locker room. As the door slowly closed behind him she sank down onto the bench and let out a long, slow, breath.

Jacob knew. And it had been every bit as horrible as she'd feared.

She felt she should have told him when she'd had that moment in Resus. Perhaps it might have gone better? If she'd been honest with him when she'd had the chance? But, no, she hadn't said anything. Instead, she'd sneaked away like a frightened mouse. And now look what had happened.

She'd *wanted* to tell him. She'd wanted to tell him ever since she'd discovered she was pregnant! But...

She hadn't been able to find him. She'd blamed him for being untraceable.

She'd wanted Seb to have it all! A mother *and* a father. As she'd *never* had. She'd promised herself that when-ever she had kids her children would have the firm foundation of a loving family. Of growing up surrounded by love and security.

When she'd realised she couldn't trace Jacob she'd quickly accustomed herself to the idea of raising Seb alone. Of relying only on herself—the way she'd always done! Seb would be able to rely on her. She'd be the best mother she could be. Her child would have the certainty that she was there to stay and she would love him more than life itself. Do the job of both parents.

Her feelings for Jacob she could control. What had they been but fantasy? He was a man she'd been able to put on a pedestal because she hadn't known him long enough to discover otherwise. Who knew what he was really like?

She could *do* this.

It would be easier now. They would be able to work together and she wouldn't have to worry anymore about him finding out about Seb. The worst was over.

Wasn't it?

She caught her own worried gaze in the mirror. Maybe it wasn't. Maybe Jacob would let Seb get to know him and then he'd disappear again? He had a temporary post here—perhaps he'd be a temporary father?

Eva got up and went over to the sinks to splash cold water on her face. She stared again at her reflection in the mirror, dabbing her skin dry with the paper towel.

'Jeez…you really didn't handle *that* very well at all,' she told herself, trying out a tentative smile.

That was better. She needed to look human again before she went to collect Seb. She didn't want him to notice she'd been crying. After today he needed to see his normal mum—the one in control. The one who soothed his brow when he was sick…the one who read to him at nights until he fell asleep. He'd need everything to be normal after the frightening start to his day in the minibus.

But I'm going to have to tell him about Jacob...

Exactly how *did* you tell a three-year-old about his father? Would he even be able to understand what she was telling him? Or would he accept it easily? In her experience her little boy was very adaptable. Maybe he'd take it in his stride?

She threw the paper towel into the bin and continued to look at herself in the mirror. She blinked quickly. The redness in her eyes was almost gone now. By the time she got out there to Seb she should look fine.

Eva opened the door.

Seb was still in his cubicle, but Jacob was with him, holding on to Seb's little fingers as he spoke to him. Seb looked intrigued. So happy. She wondered what they were talking about. She watched them together. The way Jacob spoke, the way he laughed—he was so like Seb. And Seb looked *so* like his father, with his wavy dark hair and intense blue eyes. They were the spitting image of each other. He was so obviously Jacob's little boy.

And I didn't persevere in trying to find him. I should have! We could have had everything we ever wanted...

Yeah, right. As if *that* would ever have happened...

Seb spotted her and waved. 'Can we go home now?'

Jacob didn't smile at her.

'Soon. We need to stay for a while so the doctors can keep an eye on you.'

'Because I banged my head?'

'That's right.' She glanced at Jacob.

He looked to his son. 'You know what, Seb? I'm going to come round to your house tonight. Is that okay?'

Seb nodded emphatically. 'Yes! You can tell me more about lions.'

He smiled. 'I will. I'll tell you anything you want to know.'

Eva stared at him hard, but he looked away from her and down to his son, ruffling his hair.

He'd kept them there as long as he could, but eventually Jacob had watched as his son and Eva left the department.

Hell of a first day!

He'd expected fireworks. He'd expected ups and downs. But not this. Never this!

Three years. He'd been a father for three years. Years that he'd spent in Africa, tending to the poorest and sickest of people, with almost no modern medical facilities. Watching people die needless deaths, getting depressed, drinking too much...

Thank goodness he'd stopped with the alcohol. That had been a stupid path to go down. But what with Michelle and The Wedding That Never Was, he'd felt entitled to a drink. And the drink had helped numb his thoughts. About Michelle. About Eva.

She'd been the last thing he'd expected at that party.

He'd gone there expecting to say goodbye to a couple of friends—people who had been there for him after Michelle, who had let him crash on their floors despite the stuff going on in their own lives—and there she'd been. Standing on the far side of the room, in a dress that hugged in all the right places. That flaming red hair had made her stand out in a room of mousy browns and she'd had the bluest eyes he'd ever seen, her lips curved in a half-smile.

Something about her had intrigued him.

Who *was* she? What was she doing there?

The very fact that he'd actually been thinking those questions had woken something in him. Something that he thought had died along with Michelle. And when he'd held her in his arms to dance, her soft curves moulded into his body, as if she'd been carved specifically for him, he'd turned to mush.

He'd wanted to kiss her. Had wanted to taste her. Possess her. All other thoughts—all the pain, all the grief, all the torment that he'd spent months trying to get rid of—had suddenly dissipated.

All there had been was Eva.

And she'd kept quiet. Not told him he was a father. Not tracked him down. If she had he could've been… He could've had…

He shook his head to clear his thoughts.

She was doing it again. Muddling his mind. What *was* it with women who did this?

He had to think clearly again. There was a reason he didn't like to revisit his past.

Jacob strode back into the department and picked up a patient file. No matter what, life was now going to be different. He'd get to know Seb. Slowly. Not rush it. He'd get to know his son. Let Seb get to know him. *Do I want to see my family again?*

The last time had been on his wedding day. The day that Michelle had died. Almost five years ago.

Since then, he'd been running. Running from his family…running from those who said they loved him because he couldn't cope with them. Couldn't think about dealing with their pity and their sympathy and their sad looks, their supportive pats on his back. He'd not wanted to face any of that. Nor would they have wanted to give it if they knew the whole truth of what had happened that day…

But he could be different now. Couldn't he? It wasn't just him anymore—he wasn't alone now. He had a son, and his son would need him. He refused to let Seb be without his father for a moment longer.

And it was nearly Christmas. Traditionally a time for

family. Perhaps now was the time for him to start building some bridges? Maybe let his parents know about Seb? Maybe Eva would let him take Seb for a visit? They'd love that. Love Seb. And Seb would love Jacob's old childhood home. The smallholding. The animals there. The old orchard where Jacob had spent so many hours himself.

I can't go. There are too many memories there of Michelle...

It was too much to think of going there.

Michelle had grown up right next door. His English rose, with her gorgeous straw-coloured hair that had floated and billowed in the breeze. He could picture her everywhere there. In the orchard. The barn. The house. He could hear her laughter even now, as she danced away from him, always out of reach.

His parents' grief and Michelle's mother's grief would be too much to deal with! How they all managed to still live there, he had no idea!

I bet they still have that picture of us both on the kitchen mantelpiece...

Their engagement picture. He'd felt so happy when she'd said yes.

If only he'd known of the pain she would eventually cause.

CHAPTER FOUR

TELLING SEB ABOUT Jacob was a lot easier than Eva had been expecting.

He sat there on the couch, looking up into her face with those eyes that were so like Jacob's, and she told him the momentous news.

'Seb, I want to talk to you about your daddy.'

'My daddy?'

She'd never really heard him say the word, and to hear it now felt strange. Odd. But she guessed she ought to get used to it. Jacob was back, and from what she'd seen so far he was going to stick around long enough to meet his son. Whether he *stayed* around… Well, that could be another thing entirely. When had anyone ever stuck around for her?

'Yes. You know the man today at the hospital, who helped glue your head?'

'Yes.'

'Well, that was him. That was your daddy.'

Seb seemed to think about it for a moment, his head tilted to one side and his eyes screwed up with concentration. Eva knew she had to say something else to make things clear for him.

'Daddy has been working away since you were born, Seb. In Africa. Remember he told you all about the lions? Well, he was doing very important work, being a doctor like Mummy, so he didn't get a chance to meet you. But now he's back, and he's excited to get to know you, so tonight he's coming to see you.'

'Okay,' he said, and simply went back to watching his television programme.

Eva sat next to him quietly. Waiting to see if he'd say anything else. Ask anything else. But Seb seemed engrossed.

Assuming he was fine, she got up and went into the kitchen. She was thrilled he'd taken it so well, but children were very accepting, in her experience. Until now she had been all that Seb needed.

Eva knew what it was like not to have parents. Growing up in the foster system had been a lonely experience. Some places she'd stayed longer than others, but as she'd been pushed from pillar to post she'd always felt alone and separate. Dependent only on herself for her own happiness.

She'd got used to not relying on other people. Used to people walking away. And she'd known that those who did stay, stayed only until she was sent elsewhere. She'd been a foster child. The families she'd gone to had known she wouldn't be staying forever, so there had always been that detachment. They'd never got close. Never cared for her too much, or loved her too much.

She never got attached to anyone. There was no point. The only person she'd allowed herself to love was Seb, and he meant the world to her. If Jacob was here for now, then great. But she knew she had to hold a piece of herself back from him. A piece of *Seb* back from him.

Just in case.

Because what had life proved to her so far? People pretended they were going to be there forever. Some would even promise it. They'd promised Eva that she would never have to get used to another home ever again. And what had

happened? Real sons and daughters had been born and suddenly she'd been cast out. They'd sit her down, then have
that talk with her about how things weren't working out.

There was no point in getting attached to people.

They just let you down.

And she'd promised herself—and Seb—that if she ever
did meet someone she thought could be the great love of
her life, then that person would have to love her and Seb
100 percent. She refused to be anyone's second best. Refused to be the 'reserve' love interest.

Eva spent the afternoon getting the place ready for Jacob's
arrival. Due to her working full-time, and being a single
mother, the house wasn't as presentable as she would have
liked. There were stray plastic bricks and action figures
everywhere. There was even a platoon of storm troopers
guarding the bottom of the stairs.

She cleared away what she could and vacuumed
through, polished and cleaned. The Christmas tree was
looking a little sad in the corner, so she rearranged some
of the ornaments and switched on the lights to give it some
life. She laid the dining table with her best china, in case
he stayed long enough to sit and eat with them. She cleared
the hallway of coats and shoes.

It had become a veritable graveyard of outdoor stuff,
even though there was just the two of them, but there was
a mix of wellingtons, work shoes, Seb's shoes, trainers and
slippers there, all waiting to be tripped over.

She was quite pleased with how neat it all looked when
it was cleared away. She'd never been much of a house-
keeper, having never had a real home except for this one,
and she did her best.

Now, the big question was whether to get dressed up
for Jacob's arrival?

If she tried too hard he'd know it. If she dressed casually would that take away from the enormity of the occasion? But didn't Seb need as much as possible to stay the same?

She certainly didn't want Jacob thinking she was dressing up especially for *him*, so she decided on casual. After a quick shower, she dressed in blue jeans and a fitted white T-shirt. Over that she wore a short taupe cardigan. And even though she'd decided not to make herself up especially for Jacob she painted her toenails, because she liked to go barefoot in the house. After a quick blow-dry of her hair, a swipe of mascara, lip gloss and a squirt of perfume, she felt ready.

Two minutes before six the doorbell rang.

Eva swallowed hard and felt her already jangling nerves turn into a cacophony of chaos.

He was here.

Seb's father.

'It's him! It's him!'

Seb rushed past her to get to the door first and she followed sedately after him, to give herself a few last seconds of trying to calm her nerves. She almost felt as if she was walking up to the gallows. She had no idea of how Jacob would be with *her*, but she hoped he would be pleasant in front of Seb.

The mirror in the hall told her she looked just fine. If a little apprehensive...

Seb pulled open the door and beamed at his father. 'Hi.'

'Hello, Seb.' He stood in the doorway, wearing jeans and a T-shirt with a black leather jacket over the top.

She was glad he'd chosen casual, like her, but *his* casual managed to look oh-so-sexy.

In his hands he held a gift-wrapped present, which he handed to Seb. 'This is for you.'

'What is it?'

Seb gave it a shake and Eva recognised the sound of many somethings with many pieces waiting to be built—or eventually, knowing them, sucked up into her vacuum cleaner.

'You'll need to open it to find out. Hello, Eva.' He was now looking at her, his gaze intense and unreadable.

She had to be welcoming and friendly, especially in front of Seb, so she smiled. 'Jacob. Come in. It's cold out! No need to stand in the doorway.'

She held the door open for him, inhaling the scent of him as he passed, the smell sending her back to that night she'd spent naked in his arms, writhing and tingling and gasping her pleasure...

She blinked rapidly. 'Go straight through. Seb, why don't you show your daddy into the lounge?'

She closed the front door and watched Jacob and his son disappear into the room ahead of her.

Get a grip!

She let out a harsh, short breath, then squared her shoulders and headed into the room with them.

Seb was ripping off the wrapping paper on the parcel to discover a large jigsaw puzzle of his favourite cartoon characters. He dropped to the floor in delight so he could study it better.

'You bought him exactly the right thing. He loves jigsaws,' she said, glad she hadn't already bought it and put it under the tree.

Jacob knelt on the floor and watched his son. 'My sister has a son. I tried to remember the sort of thing he was into at this age.'

At the mention of his sister, of Jacob's nephew, Eva felt chastened. She stood in the doorway, not sure what to say next.

Seb looked up from his present and beamed a smile,

then ran over to Jacob and threw his arms around his father's neck. 'Thanks, Daddy!'

Jacob looked surprised at how easily Seb was being with him, then relaxed and hugged his son back. 'No problem.'

Seb let go, and then took a step back and looked at his father. 'I'm Seb.'

Jacob smiled. 'I'm your dad. Pleased to meet you.'

They shook hands, and then Seb giggled and went back to his puzzle.

Jacob looked up at Eva and smiled hesitantly. 'He took it well, then?'

'Yes. Easier than I expected.' She sat down on the couch near him. 'It's been a big day for him, what with the accident this morning and then you. I'm sure all his questions will come later, when it begins to sink in.'

'I'm sure they will, too. He's still okay? After this morning's accident?'

She nodded. He seemed fine.

'Hey, Seb… Want me to help you do it?'

'Yes, please!'

As they huddled together on the carpet, with Jacob pretending to struggle to find pieces, she watched him—this man who had fathered her child. She'd always wondered what he would be like with his son, and here he was, playing it out live in front of her. Jacob seemed at ease with Seb, which was good, and Seb, in turn, seemed comfortable with Jacob.

Eva headed into the kitchen to make them all a drink.

She made up a tray of tea for the two of them, including a real teapot, and a juice for Seb, before heading back out into the lounge. She put the tray down on the coffee table and asked him whether he'd like sugar and milk.

'Milk without, thanks.'

She poured the drinks and sat back.

It was strange. It was almost as if they weren't strangers at all. Seb was laughing and chatting with Jacob, trying to show him how the pieces fitted together and which pieces matched which, and Jacob was laughing and smiling, and it was like watching friends who had known each other for years.

She almost felt like an outsider. The way she had felt as a foster child. Being apart from the family unit, as if she was a visitor.

Her stomach coiled in on itself at the too-familiar hurt and, feeling uneasy, she decided to interrupt. 'Is there anything you want to ask?'

Jacob looked up at her, as if he'd forgotten she was even in the room. She saw him look her up and down and then away. 'I…er…have a lot of questions, actually.'

'Okay. Fire away.'

'You were on your own? For the pregnancy? How did it go?'

She nodded and took a sip of her tea. 'Yes. Totally on my own. When I found out I was pregnant I was shocked. The doctor said I was about two months gone, and pretty much after that the morning sickness started.'

'Was it bad?'

'Pretty bad. I was okay in the mornings, but late afternoons and evenings were the worst—which weren't great whilst I was working shifts at the hospital and getting tired.'

'But you coped?'

'I always do.'

He looked at her then, his eyes holding hers just for a moment longer than was comfortable. 'Any cravings? My mum craved apple pie and custard with me.'

She shook her head. 'No. Not really. But I couldn't stand

the smell or sight of blood...which isn't ideal for an A&E doctor.'

He smiled as he clipped his jigsaw pieces together. 'What did you do?'

'I made sure there were plenty of those cardboard sick bowls in the room with me and got on with it. I wasn't going to have the hospital make special provisions for me.'

'Why?'

'Because I wasn't special.'

She wasn't going to tell him the real reason. That when she was growing up no one had ever made special provisions for her. That she was the one who made provisions for others. Fitting in around everyone else. She'd never received special efforts from anyone. Why would she have expected her colleagues at work to do that?

'And the birth? How did that go?'

Seb looked up. 'Mummy borned me in the water.'

Eva smiled. 'That's right, Seb. It was a water birth. After an extremely long and tiring labour.'

'How long?'

'Forty-two hours.'

'Ouch.'

'Ouch, indeed.' She smiled at him.

He was smiling, too.

When they realised they were smiling at each other they stopped, Jacob looking back down at the jigsaw pieces and Eva down at her cup.

What was she *doing*? She wasn't meant to be getting friendly with him. She was just meant to be polite. For Seb's sake. Nothing else was going to come of this.

'And...er...he was healthy?'

'Very healthy. Nine pounds in weight. Were you a heavy baby?'

'No. A seven-pounder. You?'

'I don't know what I was.' She could see he looked confused. Most people knew how heavy they were when they were born. Their parents usually told them. But she didn't have that information. Had never thought to ask for it, either. 'I didn't have parents,' she explained. 'I grew up in foster care.'

'Mummy had lots of homes!' Seb said, passing Jacob a piece he needed to complete the corner of the picture.

'I'm sorry to hear that.'

He sounded it, too. Genuinely. Which made her look at him carefully. He really had a kind face. It was easy to see in the wide openness of his eyes, the laughter lines around them and the generous smile of his mouth. His features were soft and rounded. There were no sharp lines, no bony angles, no harshness to his features.

She'd always believed you could see the kindness of a person in their face. If someone was a nice character, kind and gentle, then you could see it. But if someone was cruel or nasty or vicious, then you could see that, too. The meanness would be plain to see.

Jacob had a good face. A beautiful face.

And she felt a small amount of hope. That he would be a good dad to her son and remain that way. Seb deserved it. Not that she'd ever let him want for anything. He wasn't spoiled. But he *was* loved. And he knew that he was loved, and she'd tried to love him enough for two. Her guilt at not being able to give him the father he needed had hurt for a long time. But he did have *her*. He had his mother. Which was more than she had ever had.

Jacob hadn't known about his son for three years, though! He'd missed so much! How could she ever make up for that?

'I'll just check on dinner. Would you like to stay?'

Jacob looked up at her…*so* delectable. Heat flooded her cheeks at the thought.

'That would be nice. Thanks.'

'It's just pasta. Crab linguini. Is that all right with you?'

Jacob smiled. 'That would be great. Anything you're having will be fine.'

At that moment he looked so charming and approachable she had to remind herself that even though she'd once slept with this man, made a child with him, they were still strangers.

It was hard for her to get up and move away from them, from their sudden cosy family unit, to go and cook the pasta. But she figured she needed to leave them—to give them some time together without her there. A bit of father and son bonding.

Just cook the pasta. That's all you have to do.

She was successful at that, then hurried to the fridge to prep the crab. She mixed the crab meat with fresh herbs, salt and pepper and a small amount of chilli. It was good to be doing something with her hands, because before she'd been beginning to feel like a spare part. Now she felt useful. As if she was contributing.

She figured she'd better get used to it, because there were bound to be more meetings like this as Jacob and Seb got used to one another. They had so much to learn about each other. Three years of catching up to do.

How many times were you meant to apologise to a man when you'd kept him from knowing his child?

She felt incredible guilt. She'd apologised, but now she was trying to put everything right. But there was no need for her to feel beholden to him. They were both at fault for Seb not having had his father around.

The fork she was using slipped from her fingers and

clattered to the tiled floor. Sighing, she bent to pick it up—
but Jacob got to it first.

She'd had no idea he'd followed her to the kitchen and
she was surprised and shocked to find him there.

So close…

They stood up together and he held the fork out for her
to take.

'Thank you.' Her fingers brushed his and she tried not
to show how much his contact affected her.

Such an innocent, brief connection.

But such an effect.

Her heart pounded—so much so that it sounded as if it
was in her ears and not her chest. Her mouth went dry, as
if she'd spent months in the desert, and she fought to stop
her hands from trembling as she put the fork into the sink
and got another one.

Could he see her hands shaking?

Now was probably not the best time to pick up a heavy
pan of pasta, but it was done and she needed to drain it.
The pan wobbled slightly, but she hoped he couldn't see.

'Why don't you get Seb to wash his hands? This'll be
done in a minute or two.'

She heard him go and let out a pent-up breath. At the
same time the steam from the water billowed up around
her face as she strained the pasta.

How had it come to this? Yesterday she'd not had a care
in the world. She and Seb had been good. School was good.
Work was good. Home life was good. They'd been looking
forward to Christmas, just a couple of weeks away—Seb
praying for snow, as always.

It had all been *good*.

And yet today… Today her son had been in an accident
and had been brought to her A&E. Jacob had turned up out
of the blue. Her body had fired off little shots of adrena-

line every time he came near and now he'd discovered he
was father to her son!

How could just one day change so much?

Eva mixed in the cooked crab, then took the bowl of
linguini and the side salad into the dining room and called
them through.

Jacob came in with Seb on his back and set him down
by his chair.

'This looks great.'

She nodded her thanks and bade them sit. Seb helped
himself first, and Eva served up salad to everyone's plates
as Jacob served the pasta.

They all began to eat, at first in silence, enjoying the
food, and then Seb asked his first question of the night.

'Were there big lions?'

Jacob finished his mouthful of food before answering,
'In Africa? Yes, there were!'

'Whereabouts in Africa were you?' Eva asked.

Jacob smiled at her. 'Lots of places, but mostly I was in
the Manyara region of Northern Tanzania. Do you know
where Tanzania is?' He looked to his son.

Seb shook his head.

'It's between two countries called Somalia and Mozam-
bique. I'll show you on a map later, if you'd like?'

'And you were doctoring people?' Seb pushed a huge
forkful of linguini into his mouth, sucking up a stray strand
of pasta.

Jacob laughed. 'I was. It was a lot of hard work!'

Eva watched the pair of them talking across the table.
Seb looked so much like his father. It was hard to think
that they had only met today. They even held their forks
the same way.

Seb nodded. 'Why didn't you phone me?'

Jacob looked awkward. What would he say? Eva wondered.

'There were *some* phones there, Seb, but they were old, and lots of them were broken, so a lot of the time they were useless. And I couldn't use my mobile because… Well, there just aren't any antennae over there. I'm sorry. I would have phoned you if I could.'

Jacob glanced over at Eva and she looked down and away, thankful that he hadn't blamed her outright, in front of their son, for his not even knowing about his existence.

Jacob *would* have called his son if he'd known about him! That was what he'd been trying to say with that look. With just a single glance from those blue eyes of his.

The pasta suddenly seemed inedible to her, sticking in her throat, and she had to take a large drink of juice to wash it down. Then, feeling very uncomfortable and needing some fresh air, she quickly stood up. 'Excuse me a moment,' she said, and disappeared back into the kitchen.

Leaning back against the kitchen units, she held her hand to her mouth. Would Jacob ever let her forget what she'd done? Would he always try to punish her for not trying harder? She wasn't sure she'd be able to put up with those reproachful eyes of his for evermore…

She opened her fridge to check on dessert. The chocolate mousse was set, so that was fine. All she had to do was go back into the dining room and continue to pretend to Seb that everything was fine…

Back at the table, Jacob was showing Seb something on his phone. 'Do you see? That's my parents' place. Your grandparents. They own over ten acres there, and have it full of all the animals you'd find on a farm. Chickens, goats, alpacas…' He sounded wistful.

'What are *they*?' Seb was flicking through the pictures on Jacob's phone.

'They're like llamas.'

'Don't they spit?' Eva cringed.

Jacob laughed. 'Sometimes. But alpacas are gentler, I think. Or so my parents used to tell me.'

'Can we go?' Seb looked to Jacob, then to Eva.

Eva saw the look of joy and hope on his face. How could she say no?

It would give Seb a chance to get to know his grandparents. Now that he *had* some. All he'd ever had family-wise was her. Now he had grandparents and uncles, aunts and cousins. Seb's world was about to get a whole lot bigger. And though she'd wanted that for him, now that it was a reality she worried about it.

She'd have to get to know them. She'd have to sit in front of them and be judged. Like before. When she was a child. And she wanted no one judging Seb like that. Seb was her son. The one thing in this world that she had to protect. Jacob's family were strangers and she knew nothing about them.

'I suppose… But maybe in a few weeks? If Daddy is happy to take you?'

Jacob looked down at the floor. 'Er…sure.'

Eva could see that something wasn't right. Jacob didn't seem too keen on the idea. Why did Jacob seem apprehensive?

Seb's his son, too. Remember that.

She'd never shared her son. *Ever.* And now Jacob would introduce him to his new family. And she had no idea how far away their place was, or what type of people they were, and there was black ice on the roads. Today had proved how dangerous it was to travel.

What would they make of him? His grandparents?

What was she thinking? They'd *love* him. Of course they would! A new grandson to spoil. They'd love and adore Seb, surely. Welcome him into the Dolan fold without a backward glance.

Hopefully…

She had no idea what it was like to have grandparents. She could only imagine what they would think of *her*.

They'll judge me. Keeping their grandson from them for all these years…

Seb looked disappointed at her response. She could see he was keen to go. Jacob was staring at her.

'They *will* look after him.'

'I'm sure they will. It's just—'

'They're his grandparents.'

'I know they are. So…why don't *you* seem to want to go?'

Jacob looked down at his plate and she could see he was clenching and unclenching his jaw.

'It's a long story.'

'Well, maybe I need to hear that story before I let you take my son somewhere that might not be safe.'

'It's safe!' He almost laughed out loud. 'What…? You think there are monsters there or something?'

Eva glared at him. Talking about monsters in front of Seb! He had no idea how his son might feel, hearing his daddy talk about monsters! Seb could be terrified—Jacob wouldn't know!

'People aren't always the nicest.'

'My family are *very* nice.'

'So why don't you want to go?'

He looked cornered, looking to Seb first, then back to Eva. Eventually, he let out a breath. 'Because they don't know I'm back in the UK yet.'

'Why not?'

'I have…reasons.'

'I'd like to know what they are.'

Seb sucked up another long piece of pasta and grinned at his dad.

'We haven't spoken for a while. There wasn't a falling out—there weren't any arguments—it was just that I needed to get away for a while, and I didn't contact them or speak to them in the time I was away. The longer it got, the more difficult it became and now it's…almost impossible.'

Eva considered his words. 'You haven't spoken to them for *four* years? If there were no fallings-out, then ring them. I'm sure they'll be thrilled to hear from you.'

'I'm sure, too.'

'Yet you still haven't done it?'

'No.'

Jacob pushed some pasta round his plate. She watched him as she absentmindedly used her fork to twist and turn her own pasta. Seb was still eating hungrily. Her son's eyes were gleaming and bright, full of childish enthusiasm.

Jacob watched his son—gazing upon his mirror image, taking in all the details of Seb's face. The chicken pox scar above Seb's left eyebrow. The small mole below his ear. The light smattering of freckles across Seb's nose that were more Eva than him.

Eva thought back to when she was pregnant. Desperately trying to track him down and let him know about his child! Unable to find him. She'd been so upset at not being able to give her son his father! But he'd moved on, as people always did in her life, and the disappointment at that fact had hit her so hard. She didn't know why she'd expected it to be any different with him.

And it was then and only then that she had truly understood just how alone in the world she was…

She'd so wanted him to know! So wanted to have someone else there. To hold her hand. To reassure her that she could do this. To let her know that someone else cared about this baby with her—wanted to nurture it and love it and take care of it. To tell her that no longer would she have to walk through this world alone and on the edges of everyone else. That she would be a part of something. A team. United against the world.

But no. He'd gone. And so she'd faced it alone.

Until now.

Those two were already bonding. Quicker than she'd ever imagined. She knew Seb had been excited to learn his father was back, but she'd expected him to question it further. To hold something of himself back, taking his time to decide whether or not he could trust his father. But, no, Seb hadn't been like that at all! He was happy his father was here and he was carrying on as if they'd been together for always!

Or maybe those were her own thoughts?

While she'd carried Seb in her belly she'd tried over and over again to find Jacob. But eventually she'd had to admit defeat. As far as Eva had known, Jacob might never come back. As far as she had known his note might have been a lie—he might not have even been going to Africa, but slept with her and then disappeared because that was the type of man he was.

Though there had been that look in his eyes that had told her he was different. She'd wanted to find him—she really had—but after she'd hit that dead end…life had got in the way. Looking after herself and then Seb had taken over, and then too much time had passed, and…

She began to understand a little as to why Jacob had not contacted his family. The more time that passed, the more difficult it got. Perhaps they were more alike than she'd realised?

Eva excused herself and scraped back her chair, taking away the pasta still on her plate and then coming back

for theirs. Jacob and Seb had both cleared their plates—
a first for Seb, who usually left something. She raised an
eyebrow at his empty plate and was rewarded with a grin.

'Ready for dessert?'

They both nodded and looked up at her at the same time,
and the looks were so devastatingly identical she felt her
insides contract.

In the kitchen, she scraped the plates and put them in
the dishwasher, then she got the mousse from the fridge.
She served it into three bowls and carried it back out to
the table, serving Seb first, then Jacob. She sat opposite
and mutely spooned up the chocolate.

Normally it would have been delightful…enjoyable.
But right now, she couldn't taste anything and she might
as well have been spooning sawdust into her mouth. It felt
cloying and heavy and she didn't enjoy it at all.

Perhaps this was what second-guessing yourself felt
like? Whatever it was she was doing, it wasn't pleasant.

Somehow she finished the mousse. So did Seb and
Jacob. She took their dishes into the kitchen, only to hear
Jacob follow her in and set down the condiments he'd
brought through from the table.

'Thank you for dinner. I didn't know you were such a
good cook.'

'Well, there's probably a lot we don't know about each
other. But when you're alone you either learn how to cook
well or how to cook quick, and I never was one for micro-
wave meals.' She turned to face him and once again tried
to ignore the effect of his looks. He was effortlessly attractive and she found that annoying. Or was it the fact that
she was still attracted to him that irritated her?

The father of her child stood mere inches away, after
all this time. A man she hadn't seen for years now back,

tanned, matured and still making her nerve endings sing like a performing choral act.

The last time I saw you we were naked.

And that was the problem. She could still picture that night. Still remember the effect of his touch…still recall how he'd made her feel, how he'd made her yearn for more. How they'd made a child that night and how it had been magical.

The way he looked at her now wasn't innocent, either. Could he remember, too? Did he remember how she'd ground herself against him? The way she'd gasped in delight at his touch?

'I'm sorry, Jacob.'

He raised an eyebrow. 'For what, exactly?'

'For not finding you. For letting you work with me this morning and still not telling you until I was backed into a corner.' She bit her lip. 'I should have persevered. I should have kept trying to find you.'

He said nothing. Just stared at her. His eyes bored into her soul so intensely she got lost.

'Okay. Thank you. Seb wants me to stay for a bit longer. So I can be here when he goes to bed and read him a story. Is that all right with you?'

She nodded. 'Of course.'

Seb's bedroom was a little boy's dream, as far as Jacob was concerned. The walls were blue and covered in lion posters. There was a small low bed, and Jacob could see tubs and tubs of toys. There was a giant beanbag in one corner, and a small desk and chair piled high with books. A garage set lay under the window and from the ceiling hung many different plane models and homemade paper chains.

Seb's room was perfect for a boy, and he could imagine what it must be like to enjoy this room as a child.

'Wow! Great room, Seb.'

'Mum painted it. I did this bit.' Seb pointed.

Jacob made a point to study the windowsill. 'You've done a great job. You sure you haven't done this sort of work before?'

'I paint pictures in nursery.'

Jacob nodded. Seb was already in his onesie and had climbed into bed. 'So what book are we reading?'

'That one.' Seb pointed at a book.

Jacob settled down next to his son and felt envious of all that he'd missed. Cinema trips, meals out, watching Seb grow… Being there for illnesses and birthdays. And for all those other times when nothing actually happened but you were just in each other's company, watching television or sitting on the sofa.

Christmases…

All those magical times he'd not been there. It made his heart feel leaden even to think about it. But was it best that it had happened this way? Would he have been ready for this kind of responsibility three years ago?

Jacob picked up the book, found the bookmark and opened up the pages. 'I've not read this one.'

'We've read it lots of times.' Seb fiddled with his quilt. 'Will you go back to Africa?'

Jacob looked hard at his son and saw fear in Seb's eyes. 'I said I would, but… You've grown so big and I've missed so much…I don't want to miss a single second more.'

Seb smiled and snuggled down into his bed. 'Will you read to me *every* night now?'

'I'll try. I'd better ask your mum first—if I can come round every night.'

His son propped himself up on his elbows and frowned. 'But don't you *live* here?'

How could he explain? How could he explain to Seb

that his father and his mother had never even been in a proper relationship? That it had been one night when he'd let himself get carried away by a redhead with a body that wouldn't quit and the kind of lips that ought to have come with a health warning.

It was all too complicated. And he didn't want to blame Eva in front of Seb, either.

'I wasn't sure if your mum would have room, so all my things are at my flat.'

'But now you can bring your clothes here.'

Jacob ruffled his son's hair, marvelling at the softness of it under his fingers. 'Maybe. Settle down, then—let's read you the next chapter of this story.'

But his private thoughts lingered on how to sort out this situation between himself and Eva.

Clearly Eva hadn't told Seb the truth about their relationship. How could she? Seb was so young still. He could understand that. *He* wouldn't want to tell a child about that, either.

He'd been so apprehensive about coming here tonight. Learning about Seb had been such a shock to his system. One minute he'd been a single guy, with his only commitment being a temporary contract with the hospital, and the next, he'd found out that he was a father! And not to a baby about to be born, but to a three-year-old child!

He'd been furious after Eva had left the hospital. Livid. But then, after a bit of fresh air up on the hospital roof, other thoughts had entered his head. What if he wasn't a good dad? What if he had no idea of how to do it? It had been so long since he'd last allowed himself to care for someone. To love someone. He'd spent so long with his heart locked away in a box…

But a child needed love. *Deserved* to have it!

He wished he'd found out about Seb sooner, but there

was no way he could have done—no way he could have predicted the consequences of that night. He'd used protection with Eva. He'd only known her first name, and he hadn't taken her number or found out where she worked. It had been first names only and one hot, unforgettable night. He hadn't asked her any questions, because he hadn't needed to know.

She'd been his gorgeous redhead, his mesmerising siren, and he hadn't wanted to talk, or to think, or to second-guess. He'd wanted simply to go with the flow and enjoy the ride his body was taking him on. To allow her to soothe his soul. And though it had only been one night, it had made him feel alive once more. He'd hardly been able to believe it had made such an impact on him.

She'd filled his dreams for weeks afterwards. Every now and again he would think he'd caught the scent of her perfume, even though he'd known she was on a different continent!

He'd have had no way of tracking *her* down, the same way she hadn't been able to find him. Although he supposed he could have asked his friends. The ones at the party. Though actually they had been more friends of friends. But he could have asked them who the mesmerising redhead was, who Eva was...

Which, technically, he *had* done when he'd got back to the UK.

He shifted slightly and turned a page of the book, not really in the story, but lost in his own thoughts.

Upon his return to England he'd called a friend from the party that night. He'd asked him vaguely, as if it weren't important, if he could remember that night. If he could remember someone called Eva.

Mark had joked and joshed with him about it, and said

that he couldn't, but then later that day Jacob had received an email from him, with Eva's full name.

It had been as simple as that to find out where she was currently practising. Thank goodness she wasn't called Smith or Jones. Thank goodness she wasn't married! Because she might have been—there was no reason why she wouldn't have met someone else in the time they'd been apart. She probably wouldn't even remember him.

But he'd wanted the chance to see her again. Because for some reason—even after all those years—he'd never been able to get the image of her out of his head. She'd done something to him that night—something otherworldly that had brought him back to who he really was—and he'd wanted to feel that way again. Being in Africa had taught him that something was missing in his life—and he'd thought maybe, if he was brave enough to seek out Eva, he'd find it once more.

But he'd come back and discovered that he had a son…
Wow.

He wanted to know his son—although just looking at him it already felt as if he'd known Seb his whole life. It was like looking at a mini-me, only with paler skin and freckles.

The burden of responsibility hit him hard. A *son*! A three-year-old boy who would want to look up to his father and emulate him. Could he be that role model?

There was no question about it.

It was a tough situation, and he'd had enough of those to last him a lifetime: Michelle… The Wedding That Never Was…

Over time it had been easier to lock away his heart for good, to disappear when things got tough—to take a breather and throw himself into work until he could get his head around how he was feeling.

But finally he'd felt ready to come back. Strong enough to find Eva and to continue to be the best doctor he could be. Only now he could add another role to the one of doctor.

Father.

And he wanted to be the best father he could be...

For Seb...and for himself.

Eva had cleared away the dishes downstairs, cleaned the kitchen and sat down on the sofa, fidgeting with her mug of tea as she waited for Jacob to reappear.

This was the first night in a long time that she had not read her son his bedtime story.

Because his *father* was doing it! Jacob. The one man all other men had had to live up to. Not that there'd been many other men. Not seriously anyway. She'd had the odd dinner date, or been invited out to coffee, but she'd always stopped it at that. Though it had been nice to know that men still found her attractive, she'd made it clear to each and every one of them that it would not get serious. Because after a couple of dates they'd always wanted to get more involved in her life than she was prepared for— they'd wanted to meet Seb.

And none of them had been Jacob.

She'd fantasised about what might have been for so long—had stupidly almost fallen in love with her one-night stand and allowed herself to put him on a pedestal.

The night they'd spent together had been the best night she'd ever had. Of course she was bound to be sentimental about him. He'd made her *feel* for the first time in ages! Besides, they'd made a child together. Without Jacob there'd be no Seb. And her son was her world. By having her own child she'd discovered how it felt truly to love for the first time ever. To feel connected to another human being.

Of course Jacob had known nothing of the feelings he'd engendered in her. He'd slipped away into the night, never to be seen again.

Until today.

She'd always been sceptical about people who believed in love at first sight! What a cliché! Things like that didn't happen in real life, did they?

Only it had. She'd gone to her friend's party out of a sense of obligation, really. But once there she'd decided to live a little, to have a few drinks and, for once, to lose herself in the moment.

And suddenly, across the room, her gaze had collided with his. He'd stood there, half a foot taller than everyone else, and those piercing cobalt eyes had pinned her to the spot with their intensity.

The music had been blasting out, people had been talking loudly and laughing all around her, but, caught in his gaze, all she'd been aware of was her mystery man.

Her body had tingled with awareness, each nerve ending lighting up like a beacon. And when she'd realised he was coming across the room to her, without breaking eye contact, her limbs had turned to jelly, her mouth had gone dry and she'd had to physically remind herself to keep breathing.

Up close, he'd been devastatingly handsome. Tall, broad, athletic. A shock of dark hair. He'd lifted up a tress of her own hair, letting it run through his fingers, his gaze focusing on her open lips before he'd said, 'I'm Jacob. Dance with me?'

It was as if time had stopped. As if everyone else had no longer been there and it was just the two of them in that airless room. The heat, the lights, the music and them.

A slow tune had come on and he'd led her into the small dance space, his fingertips deftly pulling her after him, and then he'd spun her around and pulled her into his arms, so that she was pressed up close against his body, her hands against his chest, feeling his heart beat...

It had been magical! His touch... The connection she'd felt with him... As if that moment had always been meant to be. If she'd said that to anyone else they might have laughed at her, but she'd felt it to be true.

He'd held her in his arms and she'd rested her head against his chest and listened to his steady heartbeat, moving with him, against him, moulded into him, fitting into him perfectly.

And then the music had stopped.

She hadn't heard the next tune. She'd just been aware of his eyes, of the heat in his gaze as he'd lowered his lips to hers...

Even now, thinking about it all these years later, she could feel a shiver down her spine as she recalled how he'd slowly lowered his mouth to hers and finally—*finally!*—claimed her lips for his own.

That soft, gentle kiss had turned into a hungry demand for more, and with her silent consent he had led her out into the candlelit garden and found a summer house.

After closing the doors they'd ripped at each other's clothing, tossing it to the floor, and tumbled onto the futon inside, a mass of laughter and limbs. And then he'd taken her, his mouth insatiable as he'd tasted every inch of her, making her writhe and contort and gasp his name. She'd unashamedly clasped his hair as he'd tasted her intimately, and when he'd kissed her again she'd tasted herself on his lips. The taste, the scent of their sex had driven her on, and she'd clambered on top of him, riding him so forcefully and so deeply she'd noticed bruises on her knees days later that had made her smile with the memory of their night.

Afterwards they had lain side by side on the futon,

laughing and giggling into the early hours. Eva had fallen asleep briefly, and when she'd woken Jacob had been gone. His clothes had been missing. Her own naked body had been covered by a crocheted throw.

She'd found a folded note on the pillow next to her.

Had to leave. Africa calls!
You were amazing!
Love, Jacob x

She'd dressed quickly, ashamed at what she'd done, but glad that the party was still in full swing so she could sneak out without anyone noticing.

Eva had been forlorn. How typical of her to fall for someone who had disappeared to another continent…to Africa. Unless his note had been a joke…?

But, no, he'd left without a trace.

She'd tried to forget him. To forget that night. But then she had discovered that she was pregnant.

She hadn't believed the little blue cross at first—they'd used protection; there was no way she could be pregnant, and from one night, too.

Abortion had never been an option. She hadn't been able do it—she'd wanted her baby. No one else was going to make the decision for her. She would make it work—she would *have* to make it work. She would try to find Jacob. Try to track him down. How hard would it be?

Eva had craved to hear Jacob's voice, to feel his touch upon her one more time. She'd cried when he'd not been there to see the first scan, or to help her with nursery decoration ideas, or to help her through her contractions during labour, or to be there to hold his son after he was born. But as time had passed it had become easier. She'd become more able to bear the pain and the longing.

Until now.

And she could still feel that pull. That pull of attraction that hit her low and deep in her gut each time she looked at him. That *need* she had for him—still with her after all this time. How *could* he still have that effect on her? How did one man hold such sway over her emotions? It was like living in an emotional pinball machine, being ricocheted from one feeling to the next—fear, excitement, doubt…arousal.

But what was going on with his family? Why had he been out of contact with them for so long?

When he'd first found out about Seb he'd said to her that one of the worst things she'd done was to keep Seb from the family who would love him. Adore him. Jacob had given her that whole speech about uncles and grandparents and cousins. And yet he showed obvious reluctance to connect with that family.

Why?

She didn't need anyone else's drama. She didn't need anyone else's family issues impeding on the life she lived with Seb. They had a good life—a happy, stable life. She didn't need to take Seb down that road. The road of being judged and found wanting. Of being rejected. She wouldn't allow it.

What were they talking about up there?

She longed to be able to hear. But then she heard Jacob's footsteps on the stairs, and soon he was standing in the doorway, looking as irresistible as when she first saw him.

'How did it go?'

'He's asleep.'

'Good.' She smiled.

Jacob perched on the edge of her sofa. 'He wants to know why I'm not living here.'

Her breath caught in her throat. 'And what did you say?'

'Just that all my things were at my flat.'

'I see…' That was a difficult one.

'He wants me to read to him every night. Would that be okay? To come round in the evenings?'

That could be awkward. 'Erm…'

'I've missed enough nights, don't you think?'

'You'd practically be living here.'

'Just when my shifts allow? If it's really late maybe I could sleep on the couch?'

She'd never get a wink of sleep, knowing he was so close!

'I don't know…'

'I think we should do it. For Seb. I'd do anything for him. Now that I know I have a son I'm not going to let him down. If he wants me here every night, then I'd like to be. I'll keep out of your way.'

She stared back at his beautiful blue eyes. *How?* How would he stay out of her way? The place wasn't that big.

'Okay.'

Had she really just said that?

'Thank you. I'll go home tonight, but I'll bring a few things over tomorrow for when I have to stay.' He attempted a smile. 'I promise my toothbrush won't take up too much room.'

'Right…'

This was all moving so fast! The man she'd wanted for the past four years was practically moving in!

Jacob closed Eva's door behind him and let out a big sigh into the cold night air. The evening had gone better than he'd thought it might. He hadn't been sure how Eva would be with him. Whether she'd be treading on eggshells around him or whether she'd have loads of questions that he just wasn't ready to answer yet.

About that night. The one they'd spent together. About him leaving and never saying goodbye.

She had every right to challenge him about it. He would in her position. There was plenty she could choose to ask about, but she'd not said a thing. She'd given him the time and space he'd needed to be with Seb, and for that he was grateful.

Seb was a great kid, from what he could see. Eva had done a fabulous job in raising him thus far. But now Seb would have his father in his life and things would be different.

Jacob smiled as he walked to his car. Seb was a good-looking boy, with his wavy dark hair and blue eyes, and that alabaster skin. Girls wouldn't stand a chance when he was older! Eva had skin like that... The palest of skin tones, clear, unblemished, to the point where it almost didn't look real. The type of skin you wanted to reach out and touch, just to make sure.

He'd known he was going to find Eva in that A&E department. And, yes, he'd wanted to know more about her. There was something about her that called to him, as if she was some sort of siren singing an enchanted song that only he could hear. He'd never stopped thinking of her in Africa and that had scared him. How could a one-night stand feel like so much more?

What if they became close? What if they had a relationship? Could he keep himself emotionally separate?

Not from Seb. Seb was his son, and already he could see how easy it was going to be to love that boy, and he'd protect him to the ends of the earth if he had to. But Eva? What would happen there?

She'd already got under his skin. She'd ignited something in him that he hadn't felt for a long time. And the last time he'd felt that way... Had *thought* he felt that way...

No…I don't want to think of that anymore.

Could he even trust his own judgement? How could he know that he was making the right decisions? When he'd trusted himself before he'd been blind to what had truly been going on…

He closed his eyes and pictured the way Eva had moved that night. The way she'd felt on top of him, writhing and sweating as he'd felt himself deep inside her, as she ground him into her with a steady, yet deep rhythm. How it had made him feel to hear her gasping, to feel her hot breath blowing into the side of his neck, her fingernails scratching into his back as she'd clutched him to her as if she'd never wanted to let go…

That night had been amazing. But then he'd watched her fall asleep, her back to him, and he'd felt immense guilt, knowing he was going to have to slip away to catch his flight.

He should never have slept with her before he left for Africa. He should never have slept with *anyone*. He'd known he was leaving in a few hours and he'd not been in the right headspace—so what the hell had happened?

He hadn't even considered how she might feel afterwards. That she might feel used or abandoned when she woke up alone.

No. That wasn't true. He *had* thought about it. Worried about it. Had felt guilty about it. He'd treated her badly. Should have told her the truth from the start. He'd never forgive himself for that, even if she did.

But now he needed to be the best father that Seb could ever have. To be there always for his son. Never to let him down. Never to make a promise that he couldn't keep. To make Seb feel cherished and adored by *both* his parents.

He could do that.

Easily.

But he'd treated Eva badly once before—how would he know not to do it again? Perhaps if he stayed away from Eva and focused just on Seb, then that would be safer for them all?

He'd once felt this way about Michelle. A deep-down attraction that had pulled at his very being. And look how wrong *that* had turned out to be.

She'd seemed a safe option. The girl next door…his childhood sweetheart. Michelle had seemed so right. And yet it had all gone wrong! She'd professed to love him, professed to be true to him, and she'd ended up sleeping with somebody else. His friend! The one person he should have been able to trust most.

It had been a huge shock. Yes, Michelle had seemed more and more distracted, but he'd put it down to the wedding and how all the preparations had needed so much organising. Brides were *meant* to worry about their weddings—he'd thought her preoccupation was normal. But it had been something else…the sordid details of which she'd finally disclosed to him on their wedding day.

He hadn't seen Michelle's affair coming… Could he trust his instincts now?

CHAPTER FIVE

EVA HAD BARELY been at work for five minutes before Sarah found her and turned her round in her chair.

'So how's Seb?'

Eva thought about how best to answer her. He'd had a few aches and pains this morning, a bit of a headache, but generally seemed fine. In fact he'd seemed more than fine, and she put that down to the fact that he'd spent a few hours getting to know his father.

But did she want to tell Sarah that Jacob had been round at her house last night?

'He's good, thanks.'

'No after-effects from the accident?'

'Nothing much.' She smiled and tried to get on with her work, but Sarah wasn't going to let it go. Apparently her questions about Seb were only a preamble for her questions about Jacob.

'And Dr Dolan?'

Her fingers froze above the keyboard. 'What about him?'

'Well, you never did get the chance to tell me how you know him.'

Eva looked about them, to make sure no one else was listening, but the only witnesses were the Christmas decorations, already wilting.

'He's…um…Seb's father.' She looked up guiltily at her friend, hoping and praying that she wouldn't over-react whilst they were at work.

'Seb's dad? Really? Wow, you kept that one quiet.'

Eva nodded, her cheeks aflame. 'And there's more to it than that. I, er, only told him about Seb yesterday.'

'What?' Sarah looked totally amazed, her eyes wide, her mouth gaping, until she closed it promptly. 'What did he say when you told him?'

'He was…shocked.'

'I bet. What did he say?'

'He said I had to tell Seb. That he was going to come round.'

'And?'

'And what?'

'How did it go?' Sarah asked, as if she were an imbecile.

'Fine.'

'Fine? What? That's *it*? No furtive, lingering looks between the pair of you? No unfinished business?'

'We finished our business nearly four years ago. All that matters now is Seb.'

'But aren't you going to find out if he's single?'

Eva frowned. 'Why?' There was no point, really. It would be too much to expect that life would actually start working out well for her. That they could be a happy family unit with Jacob. *Hah!* As if *that* was ever going to happen.

Sarah shook her head in disbelief. 'Because *you're* single, Eva! And don't forget…he's hot.'

'He's unreliable. Disappears when you want him and leaves no trace. It was like trying to track down a spy. And he's only here temporarily. Once his contract is over he'll move on and we'll never see him again.'

She felt awful for saying it, but it was what she truly expected. No one ever stuck around for her. No one ever wanted to keep her in their life. Why would Jacob be any different? No matter how much she wanted him to be.

Sarah picked up a treatment card for the next patient. 'If he really was a spy that would make him hotter.'

'You're incorrigible!' Eva laughed. 'Why don't *you* get a boyfriend so you can stop trying to fix me up?'

'I'm married to my job.' She skipped off without a backward glance and left Eva pondering over Jacob.

What did she really know about him? Okay, so he was a doctor—which gave him brownie points from the get-go, didn't it? His interest in medicine meant that he spent his day helping people, and he'd even flown off to a developing continent and offered to help people there, in what must have been difficult conditions. He'd discovered that he was a father and, after his initial shock, had showed up, played with his son, eaten with them and read Seb a story. He'd even promised to come round every night, when he could, so there were signs of commitment there…

But he *had* seduced her and then left without a trace. He'd given her the barest information about himself, so that she'd been unable to track him down. Although she'd *known* it was going to be a one-night stand. She'd *known* it was going to be a one-time thing. But it hadn't mattered. She'd wanted it as much as him—had succumbed to their primal connection and lost herself in the moment.

She'd wondered then, as she had many times since, what had been driving him that night. And what had he been running away from…? She'd seen that he was in pain emotionally. In some torment. And rather than scaring her off it had drawn her to him. Two damaged souls merging together, soothing each other, before they parted ways, never to see each other again.

Although now she knew that he had turned his back on his family—but why?

He had family who cared about him—he'd mentioned that earlier, and that there hadn't been any huge falling-out. But he'd stayed away from them when quite clearly they would have supported him through whatever it was. And if there *was* something he was still running from, was he the sort of person she wanted around her son? Did he flee when the going got tough? Should she be letting Seb get to know him? Because if Jacob was going to bolt then she needed to know.

She brought up the staffing schedule for the day and saw that Jacob was supposed to be at work in Minors again today.

I need to get on with my work. I can talk to him later.

She picked up her next patient file and headed off to call the patient through, but as she walked through Minors a cubicle curtain swished open and there he was.

'Hello.'

'Hi. You okay?' he asked.

His patient smiled and hobbled past them on crutches, one ankle bandaged neatly.

She waited until the man was out of earshot. Then blew out a breath to calm herself, tucking her hair behind one ear and using the moment to try to focus.

'I'm fine. I'm glad I ran into you, though. I wanted to have a quick word about our…situation.'

'Oh…?'

She looked up into his eyes and once again found herself cursing his parents for giving him the most startling blue eyes she'd ever seen on a man. He had sickeningly long lashes, too, all dark and perfectly outlining his almond-shaped eyes. Any woman would kill to have lashes like his.

'Have you got a minute?'

'Sure. Fire away.'

'I need to know your intentions.'

He looked puzzled. 'My what?'

'Your intentions. With Seb. With the future.'

'I'm sorry, I don't under—'

'You're on a temporary contract here. For the Christmas period. I…er…I need to know if you're going to be temporary elsewhere, too.' She babbled her words, rushing to say them, to get them out of her mouth so that they wouldn't be clogging up her brain any more.

Jacob looked at her, his brow furrowed with lines.

'Are you a stable influence for me to have around Seb? Because if you're not, if you're going to disappear again, then I don't want you around him. Getting to know him. Being in his life for five minutes and then disappearing. Leaving me to handle the fall-out again—only this time with a small child in tow, who will ask questions and be hurt that his father couldn't stick around.'

He looked annoyed that she would even suggest it. 'I'm going to be there for my son.'

'Always?'

'Always.'

'Good.'

She'd believe it when she saw it. She wanted to trust him. Desperately so. But life had taught her that it didn't always work that way.

He laid a hand on her arm and looked her deeply in the eyes. 'When I came back I didn't expect to discover that I had a child. But I do, and I'm thrilled, and I'm going to be the best father he could ever have.'

She tried not to think about his hand on her arm. Warm and reassuring.

'Right. Glad to hear it.'

'Don't ever doubt me when it comes to Seb.'

She looked up into his dark blue eyes and nodded.

* * *

Somehow, magically, there was a brief lull in patients. The waiting room had almost emptied and Jacob took a brief moment to sit outside, cradling a hot cup of coffee and wrapped up tight in his jacket and scarf.

He could feel the weight of his phone in his pocket. Could feel it burning into him as he debated making that call back home. Imagining the scenarios, the conversations, the questions he would no doubt receive.

Could he face them and tell the truth finally? He'd decided in Africa that he could. But now that the time was upon him—the time to pick up that phone and make the contact that he knew his parents and family would crave—he felt anxious.

He knew they'd ask. He knew they'd want answers. So would he in their position.

I should never have let so much time pass without contacting them.

He was angry with himself for that. Angry with himself for a lot of things. He'd been responsible for what had eventually happened. He'd worked too hard, he'd taken for granted Michelle's feelings for him, and once he'd got that engagement ring on her finger he'd stopped trying. Stopped showing her how much she meant to him. No wonder she'd ended up with another man. His best friend!

That betrayal had hurt. The woman he'd professed to love and his best friend... It had been obvious afterwards. The amount of time they'd spent together... And to think he'd been so pleased that Michelle and Marcus got on so well together! Working together to plan the wedding!

I pushed them together. It was my fault.

Accepting his part in it had been a major trigger point for his coming home. He'd spent a couple of years blaming *them. Their* betrayal, *their* deceit, *their* cheating. It had been uncomfortable to turn that questioning on himself. But when he had… He'd taken some time to admit it, but he had found *himself* wanting. Had accepted what he'd done on their wedding day, yelling at her like that, causing her to rush off in tears, crying at the wheel…

He pulled the phone from his pocket and brought up his list of contacts. He scrolled down to M and found the listing he wanted.

Mum and Dad

Jacob let out a sigh and looked about him. An ambulance had just pulled up and was offloading a new patient, strapped to a backboard. Briefly he thought about going in to help out, but dismissed the idea.

He needed to do this. Make contact. He'd spent too long shutting the door on painful things in his past and he'd vowed to himself that when he came back from Africa he would face everything. He'd call his parents. He'd tell them the truth of what had happened that day. He'd tell them what he had done wrong. He would tell them everything…

He could imagine hearing their voices. How delighted they'd sound. He knew they wouldn't be cross. They weren't that type of people. His parents were easy-going and caring. They'd have *worried*, sure. They'd have fretted. Big time. But they wouldn't greet him with anger.

So just do it already!

He pressed his thumb to the screen and then put the phone up to his ear. He felt odd. Not nervous. Apprehensive…? But he sucked in a breath and knew he could handle this. He was ready now. He never had been before. But now he needed his family as he never had before. Now that he was a father himself. Now was the time to reconnect. Because of Seb.

'Hello?'

'Dad?'

A pause. *'Jacob?'*

He smiled. 'Yeah, Dad. It's me.'

A little boy had been brought into A&E by his terrified father. Separated from the mother of his child, he'd been looking after his son and had woken him from a sleep to find a lump on his forehead that had appeared suddenly.

Eva had called the mother in from work and the two parents had been at loggerheads from the get-go.

'You must have *some* idea, Lee! Did he fall? Have an accident? Go out on the ice?'

Lee looked utterly perplexed. 'No! *Nothing!*'

'Were you drinking again?'

Eva stepped in between them as their voices began to carry across the department. 'That's enough!' She eyed both of them, the look on her face the only warning they'd get, watching them both, making sure she had their attention. 'You can argue later, but right now we have to look after Ben. Okay?'

The father nodded quickly, the mother reluctantly, mumbling under her breath, 'I should never have trusted you in the first place.'

Eva could understand her distress. It was a mother's worst nightmare to find out that something was wrong with her child whilst she was at work. The most obvious explanation for Ben's large bump would be an accident, but Ben's father had denied that—and if things were as bad between them as it seemed from the way they were acting, she could see why the mud-slinging had begun and why the father was in the line of fire.

'Let's concentrate on Ben, shall we?'

His father gripped the handrails of the bed. 'I was with him all the time, Doctor—he didn't fall or bang his head anywhere.'

'Was there any time when you weren't watching him? Any chance he could have had an accident without your noticing?'

'No. Apart from when Ben fell asleep for a bit, and I caught forty winks myself. It's been manic recently, getting my new place ready for Christmas. But I woke up before he did and when I checked on him I noticed this lump that had appeared whilst he was still asleep.'

Strange, Eva thought. So if there was no chance of trauma, what else could it be? A sebaceous cyst? Pott's puffy tumour? A cyst was unlikely, as it would have been present for some time before becoming infected.

'Has he had a cold recently?'

The mother answered, 'For over a week. He's had a badly blocked nose.'

Eva bent down to look at her patient. 'Is your head sore, Ben?'

Ben nodded sadly.

She knew she needed a CT scan to confirm her diagnosis, but before she could say anything the parents began again.

'This would never have happened if he'd been with *me*,' the mother sniped.

'Well, you were at work, weren't you? He had to be with me.'

'I should have asked my mother.'

'I can look after my own son!'

'*Can* you? Because we seem to be in hospital—and I don't really think that means you looked after him very well, does it?'

Eva raised her hands. 'Please keep your voices down.' She stepped from the cubicle and sighed. These two parents were obviously struggling to share custody of their child.

Would she and Jacob become like that over time? Would she be ringing him, wherever he was, and yelling at him down the phone for not being there? She hoped not. All she'd ever wanted was for Seb to be happy, and having warring parents wasn't the way. She'd seen too much of that growing up in foster homes. If Seb ended up in hospital ill, she hoped they would pull together for their son and not bash heads like these two parents were doing.

Jacob seemed a reasonable man. So far. He'd promised he would stick around for Seb. But people made promises they couldn't keep all the time. If things got tough and Jacob left...

I hope he doesn't. I hope he can prove me wrong.

He was a very handsome man; she'd be stupid to think he would remain single. What would happen if he fell in love with someone? If his life was filled with someone else? Would Jacob still want to be around her and Seb? She was his past. They'd only shared a bed once. Made a child together. The likelihood of him having feelings for her was small.

She'd always, *always* been the one in control of Seb's life. Both mother and father to him. Now that responsibility was going to be shared and it scared her. What if Jacob did something wrong? Jacob wanted a say in his son's life. What would *that* be like?

She wasn't sure she could see it going well.

We need to get together and talk about this. It's all changing so fast.

But she wanted desperately for it to go smoothly. For

Seb. He was a good kid. Responsible and very mature for his age.

I definitely don't want us to be like Ben's parents.

She set her shoulders and went off to order a CT scan for Ben.

Jacob was there, waiting for a patient of his own. He took her to one side. 'We need to talk.'

'Yes, but not now. I've got a patient.'

'So have I! But I don't want to talk about this at your home, Eva. Not with Seb in earshot.'

'So you do care about what he hears?'

'Of course I care. I'm here for Seb forever. He's part of me. He's part of my life. I've just called my parents. Told them I'm back. Told them about Seb.' He let out a huge sigh. 'Big phone call for them.'

'You did?' Surprise filled her face. She wondered how they'd reacted.

'They were...very happy.'

'They were?' Eva felt a warm feeling in her gut. A small spark of happiness. She could accept that people had rejected *her* in her lifetime, but for Seb she wanted nothing but acceptance and welcoming arms.

'Yes.' Jacob nodded.

Eva looked at him, shocked at this turnaround. She hadn't suspected this. 'Big day for the Dolan family.'

He nodded and smiled. 'Yes, but telling my mum she's a grandmother again tended to make everything all right. When I rang off she was getting excited about shopping for more Christmas presents.'

'But they were thrilled?'

'Very. Although it did make me think that I need to get Seb something for Christmas, so I wondered if you'd do me a favour?'

'Depends what it is.' She smiled to show she was joking. But she did want to hear what it was before she agreed to anything.

'I don't know what he'd like, so I wondered if you'd come Christmas shopping with me? There's only a couple of weeks left till the big day.'

'When?'

'Later today?' Now it was his turn to smile. 'When our shifts are over? Well?'

She couldn't think of any reason why not. She had a good couple of hours before she had to pick Seb up from her neighbour's and she needed to go shopping herself, really. Christmas was looming fast and she didn't know when she might next get some free time. She didn't want to leave it to the last minute. Plus, it would give her an opportunity to talk to him. Learn more about him.

'Okay. I'll meet you after my shift ends.'

He drove them both into town. It wasn't too far from the hospital, but it would have been impossible if they'd tried to walk it. Once he'd found them a parking space, after circling a car park for ten minutes, they got out and headed into the shopping centre.

The first thing they heard, apart from the noise of chattering shoppers, was Christmas music. A beautiful rendition of 'Silent Night' was being sung live by a group of choristers at the base of the elevators.

The interior of the shopping centre was bedecked in beautiful glittering decorations in silver and white and an enormous tree stood at one end, festooned in white fairy lights with an enormous silver star at its apex.

'Wow! That looks amazing!' Eva gasped in wonder, instantly sucked into the atmosphere of the season and forgetting all about the pressures of work—the clock-watching, the reports to write out by hand as well as on the computer, the endless stream of patients, the sickness, the damage that people could do to one another. 'You almost forget there's life outside of the hospital.'

'There's a grotto.' Jacob pointed at a small wintry woodland display, festooned with mechanical bears and a snowy wood cabin. 'We should bring Seb.'

We.

She liked that. It sounded strange after being the only one to think about Seb. That he already seemed to see them as a family unit felt surreal. But good. Seb had loved having his daddy there last night, and Eva had to admit that she had been looking forward to him coming again.

It was nearly Christmas. And here she was, shopping with the father of her child, and it all seemed so simple and so easy—if she would just let it be that way.

'Where do you want to look first?' she asked.

Jacob pulled off his hat and gloves and shoved them into his pocket, running his fingers through his gorgeous hair to straighten it out. 'I don't know. There's just so much!'

'That jigsaw was a hit. And he likes playing football. Maybe a small trampoline?'

'I don't want to get him another jigsaw. I'd like to get him something fun.'

'Shall we just browse?'

He looked about him, overwhelmed by all the places they might have to go. 'Why not?'

They set off into a huge store that specialised in children's toys. It was so noisy in there! Filled with parents doing the same thing, along with children testing out the toys on display, watching robotic dogs and hamsters whizzing about on the floor. They sidestepped those and headed down one of the aisles, where there seemed to be an abundance of educational toys.

'What sort of things did *you* like as a child?' Eva asked.

'I played outside a lot. In the orchard. I made up a lot of my own games. Bits of wood for a sword, made my own bow and arrow—it was useless, but it was fun! You?'

Eva shrugged noncommittally. 'I never really had much. I was hardly ever in a real home for Christmas, and the children's home I kept going back to just got us practical things like clothes or shoes. I got a copy of *Black Beauty* once and I read it over and over until it fell apart.'

'I'm sorry to hear that.'

He looked it, too, but she didn't want his pity. She shrugged it off. 'It's okay. Anyway, this Christmas Seb really has a sense of what's going on and he's excited. I want to make it special for him.'

'Me, too.'

There seemed to be plenty of things to choose from. Games that would teach children about shopping, about telling the time, about learning the days of the week or the months of the year, or what the weather was like. Jacob didn't want to get his son anything like that. He wanted to get Seb something that was really fun.

'Three's a difficult age. What sort of things can he do?'

'He's very active. He likes physical things—going to the park, climbing on the frames, riding on the swings and things. I bet you made yourself a rope swing in that orchard of yours?'

Jacob laughed and nodded. It was good to see him smile so broadly. His face lit up with genuine joy and it felt good to know she'd made him feel that way.

'I did.'

'Was it any good? I've never tried one.'

'Never? We'll have to remedy that one day.'

One day. That implied he was sticking around, didn't it? She hoped so. Because she liked this. Being with him.

Shopping together for Seb. Doing stuff to make their son happy. It was like being united. Wanted...appreciated.

Valued.

It made her feel good. This had to be what everyone else felt.

They headed into another aisle that was filled with cuddly toys of all kinds. A large fuzzy lion was an obvious choice.

'We *have* to get him this.'

Eva nodded. Seb would like that. 'Good choice.'

Jacob tucked it under his arm and they carried on looking, ignoring the aisles full of dolls and anything pink. 'Unless he *wants* any of this?' Jacob asked.

'Er...no. Seb wouldn't be interested.'

'Just checking. Equal opportunities and all that...' He smiled.

She laughed and realised she was enjoying herself. Jacob was turning out to be the nice guy she'd hoped for. She was actually living one of the scenarios she'd once dreamed about. Being in that happy family unit...being that perfect family.

Almost.

She didn't want to spoil it. It felt good. Strangely comfortable. Pleasant.

They stood in the queue and Jacob paid for the lion. They headed back into the shopping centre and he bought them both a hot chocolate. They sat on a bench that suddenly became vacant, quickly slipping onto the seats before anyone else could, and watched the shoppers rushing by.

'This is nice,' Eva said.

'The hot chocolate? Or resting?'

'Resting!' She laughed and took a sip of her drink. 'No—this. All of it. Christmas shopping for our son together.'

Jacob looked at her and smiled.

He really was a handsome man and, looking at him now, she could really see how he and his son shared the same smile.

'I'm glad. You know, you've mentioned your childhood... What was it like?'

She glanced at him. 'You really want to know?'

She didn't mind telling him. It hadn't been a perfect childhood, but she'd made peace with that a long time ago. The past wasn't important now. What mattered was the future. And she didn't think he'd judge her if she told him. Being a doctor, he'd probably be quite understanding.

'I do.'

'The reality of it wasn't that great. I went to ten different foster families. Some of them were okay. One was really nice and I really didn't want to leave them. A young couple—the Martins, they were called...Sue and Peter. I really thought I'd get to stay with them. Be their daughter. But then Sue got pregnant with twins through IVF, and when she was about six months pregnant I suddenly found myself back at the children's home again.'

'That must have been difficult.'

'It was. I didn't understand what I'd done wrong.'

It was an understatement. She'd been incredibly hurt. And it had been a turning point for her. The point at which she'd decided never to rely on other people to make her happy. That she'd just look out for herself. No more performing seal acts to make potential foster carers think she looked cute and adorable. No more behaving well because the staff at the children's home had told her to. She'd behaved well before and look where that had got her!

'How old were you?'

'About nine. It was a tough time. I thought I'd done

something wrong and cried for what seemed like forever. Then I got used to not being wanted.'

'It had to have been a tough decision for Sue and Peter.'

She looked at him, searching his face for hidden meaning, but she didn't see anything. There was no guile there. He genuinely thought it must have been a tough decision for the couple. But she'd never thought of it that way. She'd only seen it from her own—hurt—point of view.

She thought of what they must have gone through now… making the decision to send her back. 'I guess it was.'

'Did you ever learn what happened with your own parents? Your biological parents, I mean?'

She sipped her chocolate. 'Wow. You *really* want to hear a sad story at Christmas time, don't you?'

'No. But I want to hear *your* story.'

He looked steadily at her and she eventually met his gaze.

'I was told that my mother was a young girl. A teenage runaway. She got pregnant, no one knew who the father was and she didn't want to raise a child on the streets. So she gave me up.'

'I'm sorry.' He looked at her with sadness in his eyes.

'It's not your fault.'

'No, but it must have been hard.'

'Not at first. I just sort of accepted the story. I've thought more about it since having Seb. I couldn't imagine giving him up. My mother, whoever she was, must have gone through hell to make that decision.'

'I think you've probably got her spirit and bravery.'

Eva smiled, then they both got up, throwing their polystyrene cups into the bin.

They wandered through a few more stores and she noticed that he kept looking at her when he thought she wasn't watching. She wondered if he pitied her. She didn't want that. She didn't need it. Pity did nothing for anyone. It certainly never made things better.

When they finally got to the last store and saw a beautiful blue-and-silver bike that was the perfect size for Seb, Jacob's face broke out into a broad smile.

'A bike for Christmas! His *first* bike. That'll be perfect.'

Eva beamed, too. 'I agree. But he'll need a helmet, too—and stabilisers.'

'You're happy for me to get it?'

She nodded and looked at him. 'I'm happy.'

Back at Eva's home, they unloaded their shopping and Jacob helped her hide the bike away in her bedroom closet, draping it with clothes for extra camouflage.

It felt odd having him in her bedroom, near her bed. In her most intimate space... With the gifts put away, they stood a few feet apart, just looking at each other.

'Well...I guess I ought to go. Shall I come back later? To read to Seb?'

'Yes. That would be great. He'll enjoy that.'

'So will I.'

She stared at him some more, her fingers fidgeting, unsure of what to do. She started when he took a step towards her. Then another. Tentatively, he reached up and stroked the side of her face.

'I've enjoyed this afternoon. Spending time with you. Being with you. Thank you for telling me your story.'

The feel of his fingers stroking her face sent tingles down her body. Her breath caught in her throat and she became hyperaware. Aware of his solid gaze, of where his hands were, how close he stood, exactly what he was doing.

'I enjoyed it, too.'

'I'd like to...kiss you.'

She breathed in, her chest feeling so full of air, so full

of hope for what he might do next, what it might suggest, she almost wasn't breathing at all.

'You would?'

He came nearer still. They were centimetres apart and she could breathe in his scent. Her body was doing something strange inside, with the excitement of his proximity. It was as if there were tumblers and acrobats in her stomach, and tiny, tiny dancers in each and every blood cell, pirouetting and twirling their way through her system. And their spinning was getting faster and faster the closer Jacob came.

Her lips parted.

She wanted him to kiss her. She wanted him to so much!

'There's something about you, Eva...'

She was hypnotised. His face was so close. His eyes were upon hers, burning her heart with their intensity; his mouth was so near, so tantalisingly near!

Was she doing the right thing? It didn't *feel* wrong... but surely this couldn't end well? Whenever she thought everything was going right for her, the world would pull the rug from under her feet.

She wanted his kiss, though. It was the way she'd felt once before. But this time there wouldn't be anyone jetting off to another continent straight afterwards. This time it wouldn't be a one-night stand. This would be something else. A couple reconnecting. A woman and a man who had already made a child together, who had been parted by geography and mileage, who could now be together. Who could be stepping towards the future together.

'But...' He reached up and threaded his fingers into her hair, his hands gently holding her face.

'But?'

'I don't want to ruin this friendship we're creating. I don't want to ruin it for Seb.'

'You won't.'

She looked deep into his blue eyes and saw his soul. He was a tortured man still. She could see that. Sense that. He carried pain within him, something he still hadn't shared with her, but she knew deep in her heart that if she just gave him some time, gave him some room to feel comfortable with her, then he would share it. And once he shared she could help him. She knew she could.

It was probably the lust talking, telling her it wasn't a problem, but she couldn't help it. Being this close to Jacob was electric.

How bad could it be? It wasn't as if he'd murdered anyone. He wasn't a bad guy. Something had hurt him. Something or someone had taken hold of his heart and crushed it.

Eva wondered if she could help him mend it. But what would happen if she did? If she let him in, if she started to care, then she would be taking a chance on him that she'd never, ever taken with anyone else. She would be opening herself up to being hurt again. There *was* that risk, wasn't there? Every other relationship in her past had failed. What would make this one so special?

But what if *this* was a relationship with the potential for something amazing?

That tantalising thought hypnotised her. Blindsided her doubt for a moment.

Jacob pulled her towards him.

Her body pressed up against his and then her eyes closed as her lips met his. Elation flooded her system with ripples and waves of intoxication as the reality of kissing Jacob again sank in.

Their shared kiss, though tender, opened up something inside her that she hadn't been expecting.

A fervour. A *need* that she'd never experienced with any man before.

She burned for him. Breathed him in. Melted into him as she felt his hands caress her and hold her against him. The solidness, the hardness of his male body against her soft femininity was a beautiful yin and yang.

The last time she'd kissed this man she'd lain naked in his arms and allowed herself to fly through the skies with him, soaring amongst the clouds and the heavens as he'd taken her to fever pitch and back again. Being in his arms again felt so *right*, and strangely so *familiar*—as if it had been seconds since they had last held her and not years. His lips were warm and soft against hers; his body was against hers… It made her come alive…

He pulled back to look at her with glazed eyes.

She had no doubt that she looked the same.

Eva touched her lips. 'Will you be with us at Christmas?'

'I'll need to see my family, too, but, yes… I'll be with you for Christmas.'

His family. The people she hadn't met yet. These strangers she would now have to share Seb with. Leave herself open to inspection from. It didn't seem too scary right now, with Jacob, but she was worried about what would happen later.

What would he be like with them? What did she know about him? Really?

Eva craved for all this to work out, but experience told her not to get her hopes up. She wanted not to be afraid. But she'd been hurt so many times before…

I want to be part of a family so much!

But did she dare hope she could actually have it?

Jacob had come back for the evening. They were sitting together in the lounge, whilst Seb played on the floor between them.

'I spoke to my parents again. Said we'd probably take Seb one day before Christmas.'

She frowned. 'Oh?'

Before Christmas? She only had one weekend free between now and Christmas, and spending it with a family she didn't know didn't sound very appealing. Besides, these people probably wouldn't even like her.

'Don't you want to take him on your own? I'm sure they don't want me hanging around—'

Jacob shook his head. 'It'll be fine!'

'No. It's probably best it's just you and Seb at first.'

'They'll want to meet you. I'd really like it, too, if you came. They're very friendly! If anyone is going to get questioned it'll be me. I'm the one who stayed away.'

She smiled at him. 'I know. It's just…difficult for me. Isn't it hard for you, too? You stayed away for a long time. Aren't you worried about going back?'

Jacob nodded. 'I am. There are lots of memories there.' He thought for a moment, his eyes dark, and then he said, 'Someone I loved…she died.'

'I'm so sorry.'

'It's fine. I've accepted it now. That's the whole thing about going back. I need to face my demons over being there again.'

'And you don't want to go alone?'

'I could go alone…but I'd like you to be there. It's not just Seb who's a part of my family now. You are, too.'

She could feel her cheeks flame with heat. 'Really?'

'Really.' He laid his hand on hers.

'Thank you. Do you…want to tell me about her?'

He looked away. 'She was a childhood friend. Someone who came to mean a great deal to me.'

She nodded. It was understandable that he should have someone like this in his past. And now she could understand some of his reluctance to go back home. It had to be a past love. A love affair that somehow went wrong, perhaps.

A tinge of jealousy announced itself, but she pushed it away. She had no right to feel jealous about this.

But was he over this woman? She wasn't sure. Obviously the pain of loss was still there. She'd seen it in him before. The night they'd met.

They watched Seb play on the floor, silent for a moment, Eva sipping at her tea and Jacob looking back at her darkly, stuck in his memories of the past.

He was hurt. That much was clear. But surely he must have moved on? She didn't want to be his soft place to fall just because he was hurt—she wanted to be his because he wanted to be with *her*. Heart, soul—everything.

Anything less was too risky.

If she suspected he wasn't over this woman then she'd walk away from a relationship with him.

Why did he have to tell me about her? It was all going so well…

Eva needed certainty in her life. Needed security. If Jacob and events in his past somehow threatened that, then she'd separate herself from him immediately. Better to keep him at a distance until she knew for sure. Better to tread carefully.

It wasn't just about *her* anymore.

CHAPTER SIX

A WEEK LATER Jacob took them some Christmas lights. Small white fairy lights to hang outside, around the guttering and over the small fence in the front garden. Eva had told him she hadn't decorated the outside of her house as she hadn't felt safe going up a ladder on her own with just a three-year-old to steady it.

That morning frost had covered everything, making surfaces slippery, and as he worked he could see his breath billowing out around him and his fingertips turning redder and redder as they lost more and more feeling. The little plastic grips that would secure the lights along the guttering were fragile, and he lost more than he used as he tried to force them onto the edge.

But he didn't mind. He felt *useful*. The past few nights when he'd turned up to Eva's home he'd noticed that she was about the only person in the street with no Christmassy outdoor lights so he'd offered to do it, knowing Seb would like it, too.

Eva stood at the bottom of the ladder, holding it, looking up at him and laughing every time he cursed as another clip skittered away from his fingers and fell to the ground.

'Will I need to get you another packet?' she asked, laughing.

He grimaced as he forced another clip into position. 'Maybe. At this rate I might start suturing them on.'

The last clip went into place and he descended the ladder to collect the lights so that he could trail them across the front of the house.

'Can you believe people go through this madness every year?'

'Christmas is a time to make everyone happy, isn't it?'

He nodded. 'Kids, maybe.'

Eva frowned. Surely *he'd* had good Christmases? 'Is Christmas not a happy time for you?'

She seemed genuinely interested in his experiences. But he felt bad about talking about them. His childhood Christmas memories were great, and he knew hers weren't. She was the one who'd been in foster care—not him. It was that one Christmas Eve he'd experienced five years ago that really bothered him.

'It wasn't for you.'

'My Christmases were…different. I ended up in so many places I lost track of all the varying traditions people had.'

'But were you happy?'

She shrugged. 'I never belonged. I always felt I was intruding on someone else's memories.'

Someone else's memories… No. He didn't want to mess with those.

'Christmas was just fine for me until a few years ago.'

He picked up the knot of fairy lights and began to untangle them, handing Eva one end so he didn't lose it.

'We made Seb on a Christmas Eve. That's a good memory, isn't it?'

His numb fingers stopped moving as he looked at her. She was bundled up tight in her winter coat, her red hair just peeking out from underneath her woolly hat, and her nose was bright pink over her thick, fluffy scarf. She looked like a model posing for a winter-clothing campaign, and he almost wanted to take a picture of her to capture the image.

'Yes. But Christmas Eve isn't all jolly excitement and meeting hot chicks at parties.'

She stared at him, amused. *'Hot chicks?'*

Jacob managed a smile. 'You *were*! I'd not expected to see anyone like you at that party. I hadn't gone looking for a one-night stand, you know.'

She looked about them to make sure there were no nosy neighbours listening in. 'I'm glad to hear it.'

'I was looking to…escape. Forget for a while.' Jacob pulled at more of the wire. 'What were *you* doing there? That night?'

'Well, I hadn't wanted to go, either, but decided to make the best of it once I got there. From what I remember, your eyes looked…sad.'

Jacob headed back up the ladder, so that she wouldn't see the look on his face. He didn't want to talk about Michelle right now. He didn't want to tell Eva about what had happened. Not yet. Not what he'd done. Because if he did then she might be horrified with him. She wouldn't see Jacob the doctor, father of her baby.

If he told her the truth she'd be appalled.

Because he'd killed a woman.

A woman he'd supposedly loved.

No one got to do that and then be entitled to happiness. This life—this chance with Eva and Seb—he *wanted* it, but he wasn't sure he'd be allowed to keep it if he told her the truth. What if he took *her* for granted, too? Or, worse still, Seb? What if they argued and she ran off? Or drove off and…?

The thought of Michelle's blood in the snow smacked him straight between the eyes.

'That someone special I told you about…she died on Christmas Eve. Each time it rolls around I tend to think about it. That night we met, the party was a great excuse for me to say goodbye to a few friends and hopefully forget for a while.'

'Did it work?'

He looked down at her from his perch atop the ladder. 'It did. I met *you*.'

Eva looked up at him and felt her heart flutter in her chest. He'd met her on the anniversary of this woman's death, and though he'd been hurt, though he'd been pained by the day, she had helped manage to soothe him—if only for a short while.

She'd always known she'd seen something in his gaze that night—before she'd spoken to him, before they'd got close. He'd been grieving! It seemed so obvious now. And they'd made something beautiful out of something painful.

They'd made Seb. And here they were, years later, together. Who knew how it would end?

She hoped it wouldn't.

The days running up to Christmas began to pass much too quickly.

Jacob spent as much time as he could at Eva's—playing with Seb, having dinner with them and then reading Seb his bedtime story. He also took him out for walks on his own.

Eva began to learn more about the father of her child—he liked reading and photography, and had taken loads of photographs in Africa, some of which she thought he should enter into competitions, they were that good. And she learned about the work he'd done in Africa—first in an eye clinic, saving the sight of thousands by performing simple cataract operations, and then he'd helped build a new school.

He was certainly handy around the house. The dripping tap in her kitchen had been fixed, and he'd shaved a few inches off a door that had never shut properly and he'd even offered to help repaint a room.

But she was wary of taking advantage of him. Of letting things move too fast. He was there for Seb, after all, not her—though they were getting along well as a unit, and she couldn't help but notice how attractive he still was to her.

Since that kiss after their shopping expedition she'd felt torn about experiencing it again. She wanted to. Very much! But she was afraid of what would happen if she did. Too many times she'd thought she could have something and keep it forever, and it would always be torn from her grasp.

It was difficult to concentrate sometimes, with him in the house. He'd be reading to her son, lying on Seb's bed with his arm wrapped around him, and she would watch them from the doorway and marvel at how homely it looked and how it made her feel all warm inside and safe. But then he'd come downstairs and put his coat on to leave, and there'd be that awkward moment at the door, when he'd kiss her goodbye on the cheek and then look longingly at her, as if he wanted to do more.

She'd been keeping him at arm's length. Trying not to let herself get carried away by his being there and the thrill of the season. Letting him know, subtly, that she wasn't rushing into anything. Believing that if she kept him at a distance she'd be able to stop the pain before it came if anything went wrong—that somehow it wouldn't hurt as much.

But it didn't stop her yearning for another proper kiss. She could feel the tingle in her lips at the idea each time he came round, wondering if maybe today he might kiss her again, but Jacob seemed determined to respect her boundaries.

And still Eva was determined to crack his exterior. To delve deep inside this man who had fathered her child and find out more about his past. She wanted to understand him. Know the pain that he carried. Because if she did then she would know if she and Seb were safe from being left behind. She wanted to know about Jacob, and the fact that she didn't know him as well as she could frustrated her.

Perhaps if she did go and meet his family then it might provide her with the opportunity she needed.

Jacob was sitting next to her on the couch. Wine had been poured and the fairy lights twinkled outside the window and, in the corner of the room, twisted around the Christmas tree.

The television had been turned off. It was just the two of them. Seb was fast asleep upstairs.

'I'm glad you came back from Africa when you did, Jacob.'

'So am I.'

'I was terrified, you know—at first, when I saw you standing in Minors that day. All I could think of was how was I going to tell you about Seb.'

He smiled at her. 'You managed it.'

Eva laughed and sipped her wine. 'Just about. What was it that made you come back? From Africa? Did something happen? To make you come?'

She watched as his blue eyes darkened.

'Something. *Someone*, actually. You have to understand I met a lot of patients over there. Heard a lot of sad stories. The people there were brave. Proud. Each one touched my heart, day after day, but there was this one story that I just couldn't get out of my head.'

'What was it?'

Jacob poured more wine into their glasses and put the bottle back on the table.

'This man brought his wife into the hospital. His name was Reuben and he was in his seventies. You could see the *life* in his face. The wisdom and the pain etched into every line. But he held himself tall and proud. His wife was dying of malaria and we watched her fade every day for about a week.'

Eva listened intently.

'Reuben told me that he'd met his wife, Zuri, when they were teenagers. They'd fallen in love, but Reuben's family had arranged a marriage for him to another woman and they forbade him from seeing Zuri. It broke his heart, but he had to do what his father ordered. He married this other woman and they had children and he said it was a good life, if not a loving one. His wife died when Reuben turned seventy, and he thought that was it for him. That he would die lonely because his children had all grown up and flown the nest. Until he met Zuri again in the market.'

Jacob smiled.

Eva smiled, too.

'Zuri had lost her husband long before. She had been unable to bear children and he had walked out on her. She'd been alone for years. But Zuri and Reuben got together and married within weeks of meeting each other again. They'd been married only three months when he carried her into my hospital, exhausted and spent. When Zuri died, just a week later, Reuben stood with me at her funeral, and he turned to me and thanked me. He said that life was short and that if I had any loved ones at home then I should return and be with them. Because you never knew when life could take them away from you.'

'Poor Reuben.'

'He told me those three months with Zuri had been the happiest of his entire life. His story stuck with me…eating away at me. I kept thinking about Reuben for months afterwards. The twists and turns of his life. How he'd ended up with the one woman he should have been with from the beginning. How he'd known it was special with her. How the short time he'd had with Zuri was the happiest he'd ever had. I kept thinking of you. Of the night we met. How it had felt…special. How you'd made me feel. I wanted to come back and find you. Tell you. See if there was something we could make of that connection we'd felt.'

Eva nodded. 'Because life is short?'

'Exactly.'

He reached up to stroke her face and she leaned into his hand. His gaze was intense as he focused on his fingers, tracing her jawline and then moving down her neck, over the pulse point there that was throbbing madly and down to the neckline of her top. As her pulse accelerated his hand dropped away and he looked up at her, suddenly uncomfortable.

'What is it?'

'Nothing.'

'There's something, Jacob. Please…please tell me. It could help.'

He still looked at her, uncertainty in his eyes.

She could tell that he wanted to say something but was afraid to. *Why?* Surely he trusted her? Had he done something terrible? Because if he had then she needed to know. Not just for her, but for Seb, too. She had to know who she was getting involved with. It was the only way to protect her own heart.

'I *want* to tell you...'

She reached over and took his hand in hers, cradling his fingers with her own, wrapping her hand over his. 'You can.'

'I've never spoken of this to anyone.'

'Then, it's time. If you keep pain inside it eats you alive, Jacob. You can't live with pain all the time. You know what they say about a problem shared?'

He squeezed her fingers. 'It's a problem halved?'

'That's right.'

He let out a big sigh and then nodded. 'A year to the day before I met you was supposed to be my wedding day.'

Eva tried not to show surprise. 'Okay...'

He let out another breath. It was clearly getting easier to say the more he spoke. 'I was getting married to Michelle. She was a childhood friend. She lived next door to my parents' smallholding and we grew up together...and then we became something more.'

Eva tried to imagine him with someone else. Loving another woman intensely enough to want to marry her. The idea of it made her feel uncomfortable.

'You loved her?'

He nodded. 'Yes. I thought so anyway.'

Eva frowned and took a sip of her drink.

'I proposed and we set a date. December the twenty-fourth. It seemed romantic. We'd hoped for snow and we got it, too. For the first time in years it came down quite thick. It had been raining the previous day, so no one thought it would settle, but it did. It made everything look beautiful.'

She could picture it in her head. 'I can imagine.'

'I was at the church, waiting. You know how brides are meant to be late? Well, I waited outside for her to arrive, thinking I'd head into the church when I saw the bridal car. She was a bit late, but I thought that was because she was getting ready on her own. She didn't have a father or any brothers to give her away. She was going to walk up the aisle alone.'

Eva sipped her wine. It all sounded lovely so far. But she knew something was coming. Something bad. She could tell from the way he was telling the story. The fact that he'd never spoken of this. She could hear it in his voice. See the pain in his eyes. The same look he'd had four years ago, when she'd met him at that party.

He looked away. 'She never made it.'

'How do you mean?'

'She was hit by a heavy-goods vehicle. Side impact on black ice. She wasn't wearing a seat belt and she was thrown from the spinning vehicle. She died on the tarmac, bleeding into the snow.'

Eva covered her face with her hands. How awful! 'Oh, Jacob, I'm *so* sorry!' No wonder he hadn't wanted to speak of this! His bride…? Dying on their wedding day…?

He wouldn't meet her gaze. He just stared at the carpet.

Now she understood. Now she understood the look that had been in his eyes at the party. The most horrific thing had happened to him. Of *course* she could understand it now. Understand why he had kept this in for so long.

But she was glad that he'd felt able to tell her. To confide in her. It meant something. That they were getting closer. That he trusted her with this information.

It all made such sense. His childhood friend, this Michelle, a woman he'd grown up with. A longtime friendship becoming something more, something more intense. Love. Commitment. And he'd lost her on what should have been the happiest day of his life!

She wondered briefly what Michelle had been like. The woman who had been Jacob's friend…who had become his love. What hopes and dreams had she had about their married life together? She would have got ready that morning, ready for church, for her wedding—and how happy she must have been.

Now Eva understood why he didn't look forward to Christmas. Why it held bad memories for him.

'Perhaps now…with us…Christmas can become a good time for you again?'

He looked at her. 'I hope so.'

'Thank you for telling me, Jacob. I know it must have hurt.' She squeezed his fingers. 'I really feel we can move forward now. I'd like to go with you to your parents' place.'

Though she still felt nervous about it—and would continue to until they'd been. Until she'd seen how his family were with her. But if Jacob could make this huge step forward by confiding in her, then she could do this for him. It would help him. Her, too. And it would give her the opportunity to learn more about this man she wanted to trust implicitly.

Jacob focused on her as she spoke, nodding. 'I'd like that. So would they.'

He continued to stare at her and she stared back. They were so close to each other on the couch. Their legs had been touching the entire time Jacob had been speaking and while they'd sipped at their drinks.

She hoped that now he had started to open up about himself he would continue to do so. Perhaps back at his childhood home, confronting old memories, he would do so. She could learn more about him. About Michelle.

What if he still loves her?

The horrible thought impeded on her warm feeling inside and she tried to crush it down. Ignore the fact that she'd thought it. But the more she tried to ignore it, the stronger it seemed to get.

Jacob had had the love of his life ripped from him! It wasn't a love that had slowly died. It hadn't ebbed away with the years. She hadn't cheated on him.

She'd *died*!

He *had* to still love her!

And if he loved a dead woman how could they ever truly be together? She wasn't going to try to compete with a ghost.

She couldn't afford to get involved with him. She couldn't risk her relationship with him. It would end badly.

Perhaps it would be best if she kept her distance from him until he'd sorted out the feelings he still had.

She looked down at his lips, at his smooth mouth amongst the small forest of stubble that grew around his jaw. A small scar marked a brief valley on his chin. How had he got that? Shaving? A boyhood accident?

What if he *wasn't* still in love with Michelle?

Would she be risking ruining their relationship by creating distance between them when she didn't need to? Would she be fulfilling her own prophecy by keeping him at arm's length?

Life is too hard!

Her gaze went back to his lips. Then to his eyes. He was looking at her so intently. All she had to do was lean closer, close the gap, close her eyes and then he would be hers...

Eva stood up abruptly, placing her wine glass on the table. 'It's nearly time for you to go.'

'Of course.'

This was best. To have the distance they both needed. *It's the right thing to do.*

So why did it hurt? Why did she want him to stay? Because if he stayed who knew where it might lead?

It was best this way. He was clearly still grieving—he

was the last person she should be letting herself get involved with right now. She knew that.

He nodded and grabbed his jacket, pecked her on the cheek and headed into the hallway. She heard the front door open and close.

She pressed her hand to her cheek. The warmth from his lips was fading away.

It felt awful to create space between them, but it was the best thing to do.

The house was normally quiet when she woke up in the morning, and she could sit and read a newspaper quietly with a cup of coffee before Seb came bouncing down the stairs, full of life and noise.

But this Saturday morning Jacob had arrived early, and the smell of frying bacon filled the house, causing her to salivate. Even though she didn't normally eat fried breakfasts—she was a cereal and half a grapefruit kind of girl—she wolfed down bacon, two sausages, scrambled eggs and toast.

Jacob was a good cook, and Seb was enjoying having his father around for breakfast.

They could talk to each other for hours, and Eva had often found herself having to grab a book and go off and read somewhere while Seb got to know his father. It was only fair after all. They had three years to catch up on, and Eva no longer felt as if she was being left out.

Jacob had learned that Seb enjoyed nursery, loved sport and animals and wanted to be a doctor one day, like his parents. Seb was also hoping for snow on Christmas Day. Lots and lots of snow. And Seb had learned that his dad had gone on safari and met a real-life leopard, seen a lion pride and even been charged at by an elephant.

It was only as they talked, as they chatted, that Eva realised they were so alike in their mannerisms. Why had she not realised that Seb rubbed at his chin when he was thinking, the same way Jacob did? Why had she not noticed that that they both stuck out their tongues slightly when they were concentrating?

Silly things. Inconsequential things. But everything she noticed was amusing and quaint. Familiar. Things *she* didn't do but Seb did. Why had she never wondered if they were traits from his father?

Jacob was clearing away their greasy, tomato ketchup–smeared plates when he asked Seb a question. 'Seb, do you remember I told that you my parents have a small farm with lots of animals?'

'Yeah,' Seb answered.

'Well, your mum and I have been thinking, and we thought you might like to visit there today. Stay the night. Get to know your grandparents and see the animals.'

Eva nodded as Seb looked to her, as if for permission. She was pleased that she'd agreed to take this step. But it was a huge about-turn for her. The idea of meeting Jacob's family had at first been scary. She'd never wanted to stand in front of strangers and be judged again. But since Jacob's revelations about Michelle, and with the way their relationship was developing, she'd begun to accept that this was the right thing to do. Especially for Seb. These people she didn't yet know were his family, and whether she and Jacob became something or not his family would always be there for her son.

This was an opportunity that she had never had. It was an enormous step forward for them both.

'Can we?'

'Course we can.'

Seb beamed a smile at them both. 'Cool!'

'We'll need our wellies!'

Eva was still anxious at the thought of meeting Jacob's parents. Even though he'd told her they were nice and friendly. They would assess her.

But she had to remind herself that she was an adult now—not a child. If Jacob's parents and family didn't like her, it didn't matter too much. What mattered most of all was that they knew Seb and adored him. If they didn't like *him*... Not possible! Of *course* they would love Seb. They *had* to.

So she was off to the Dolan smallholding. Where everyone who had no right to judge her lived. Perhaps Jacob was pleased she was going because then his parents wouldn't be able to have a go at *him*?

This weekend was going to be truly uncomfortable for her. Jacob had apparently already told them that they'd need separate beds...

Going to meet a new family again... How many times had she done *that*? Stood outside on the pavement, by a social worker's car, whilst a new family came out to greet her. Assess her. Judge her worth.

They'd all be looking at her. Deciding if they liked her or not. Deciding if she was worth keeping.

It shouldn't matter what they think. I am part of their family now. Because of Seb.

But it did matter.

It mattered a lot. She *wanted* them to like her. She *wanted* to be accepted. She really wanted to be welcomed into the Dolan family.

It was a two-hour car journey that became nearly four. Everyone was driving slowly and more carefully due to the ice still on the roads.

Eva sat in the front seat as Jacob drove them in his sleek black car, with her stomach knotting with nerves at every mile. Jolly Christmas music played over the car stereo—music that she would normally sing along to. But not today. She was a bag of nerves—as jittery and shaky as a naked person in the Arctic.

The last time she'd felt this nervous she had been taking the pregnancy test. Her stomach was clenched tight, her mouth was so dry she could barely speak and she had to keep stretching out her fingers to prevent cramp as she was clasping them so tightly.

And to think I thought I was being relaxed about this!

Outside, the world was doing just fine. Only a week to Christmas and it was a beautiful, crisp winter's day, with blue skies and bright sunshine. They passed fields of grazing horses and cattle or sheep as Jacob drove them down winding lanes through the countryside. There were some flowers growing at the roadside that she'd never seen before. Winter honeysuckle? She wasn't sure. She'd never been green-fingered.

It all looked so beautiful and serene, but as they passed a sign for Netherfield Village—the place where his parents' smallholding was meant to be—she could almost feel her blood pressure rising all by itself. The village was picture-postcard perfect. Literally, she could have taken a photo of its village square and used it as a Christmas card. It was sickeningly beautiful. The type of place you wanted to move to the second you saw it.

Jacob seemed nervous, too, as he drove. He was going home to his family, but he seemed edgy. She supposed that was to be expected. He'd been away from home for years. And he knew that by going back he'd be facing old, painful memories. She was proud of him for doing it, and pleased that he was able to do it with her at his side.

Her stomach rolled as she thought about how she'd kept his parents' grandson from them. Not deliberately—but would they readily accept the fact that she'd not been able to find Jacob? If they were going to have a go at her she hoped they'd do so out of Seb's eyeline and earshot.

She hadn't kept their grandson from them on purpose. They'd lost three years of their grandchild's life. Three years that they'd never get back. Three years of memories and photos and home videos that didn't exist because she'd not persevered in finding their son.

Had she given up too easily?

No. I tried my best.

The thought of meeting them filled her with nerves, and though the fried breakfast had seemed a wonderful idea a few hours ago she could feel it sitting heavily in her stomach now, the grease swirling around inside her like an oily whirlpool, making her feel extremely queasy.

'Nearly there now, Seb!' Jacob called over his shoulder to his son.

'Great!'

Seb leaned forward in his booster seat and looked between the two front seats through the windscreen as Jacob steered his car through the quaint village, past a pub called The Three Horseshoes, a post office, a grocery store, some quaint thatched cottages and then down another lane.

'There's the alpacas!'

'Wow!' Seb exclaimed from the backseat.

Jacob laughed. 'We keep them in the fields where we have the chickens and the geese and ducks. They keep away the foxes and my mum uses their fur to make quilts and baby blankets.'

'They keep away foxes? What? Like guard dogs?' Eva enquired.

'Exactly.'

Seb wound down his window for a better look, letting in a blast of cold air. 'They're funny!'

Eva smiled at his amusement. They were close now, and she could feel Jacob's apprehension building.

Just past the alpaca field he turned into a smaller lane, with lots of lumps and bumps. The car jolted them around as its suspension system struggled with the holey road, but then they were pulling up in front of a redbrick farmhouse with window boxes and a border collie dog lying outside, panting heavily, its breath fogging in the chill air.

'That's Lucy,' Jacob said. 'Come on, Seb! I'll introduce you!'

Father and son got out of the car and had gone over to the happy dog, making a big fuss of it, before Eva could even remove her seat belt. The dog wagged its tail madly at Jacob and lasciviously licked at Seb's happy face.

Eva took that moment to look around her.

To the side of the house there was a rotary washing line, empty and frosted, there were plant pots and tubs filled to overflowing with winter bulbs and early crocus and there were blue gingham curtains at the windows, tied back with sashing.

Eva almost expected to see a hot apple pie cooling on a windowsill!

There was a ginger cat curled up on an outdoor chair in the winter sun, and it opened a lazy eye as she closed the car door and blinked in the bright sunshine.

With the rolling fields set as a backdrop to the old redbrick house, the place was beautiful!

Seb and Jacob were still ruffling the dog's fur, Seb beaming, when the front door opened and Jacob's parents emerged from inside the house.

Eva felt her hesitant smile freeze on her face at their appearance. This was it. The moment she'd been worrying about. She looked to Jacob to see how he'd react, and saw him stand back and stare at his parents, a half smile on his face.

They stared at each other for a moment. Eva could see that Jacob's mum was dying for her son to speak, but Jacob seemed incapable of saying anything.

Needing to break the tension, Eva stepped forward, away from the car. 'Mrs Dolan?'

His mother turned.

Her son looked so like her. Jacob's mother was tall and slim and had the same dark colouring, though her hair had a grey streak in the centre, but his father was already grey haired and slightly plumper.

And they were both smiling.

'Eva!' Mrs Dolan stepped towards her and embraced her firmly, pulling her into a bear hug she couldn't escape from. 'You must be tired from your journey. We were expecting you hours ago! Come on in! We've got freshly baked biscuits and mince pies inside, and a fresh pot of tea.'

She released her and beamed a smile at her.

Eva was delighted. 'Er...lovely... Thank you.'

This was more like it! Eva felt instantly accepted! Where had *this* sensation been as a child? Where had the warm bear hugs been then? Where had the home-baked biscuits and the welcome and the *acceptance* been?

'Jacob!'

Jacob's mother pulled him to her, squeezing him tight, as if she never wanted to let him go, and then she kissed him on both cheeks and looked at him for a long time, her hands cradling his face.

'You've come *home*! You've changed...'

Then she turned to Seb and pulled him into a hug.

'And you must be Seb! We've been *so* looking forward to meeting you!'

Jacob looked relieved and managed to smile fully at last.

Jacob's father walked over and gave him a hug and a quick back slap. Then they stepped apart.

'Hi, Dad.'

'Son... Good-looking boy you've got there!'

Once Seb had stopped ruffling the dog's fur and rubbing its belly, they stepped into the farmhouse. The front door took them straight into the kitchen, which was made up of old wooden units, with dried flowers and copper-bottomed pots hanging from a rack above. There were two metallic strips on the walls, holding a line of knives and shiny utensils, and in the centre of the kitchen a huge oak table that had been laid for guests.

Candy-cane bunting decorated the walls and a huge spray of holly erupted from the vast copper pot set in the fireplace. Christmas cards lined every available surface. Clearly the Dolans were very popular people!

A vase in the centre of the table held a beautiful bouquet of pine stems, interspersed with cinnamon sticks and dried orange slices. Unusual, but very aromatic, and around it were the promised plates of pies and biscuits. A hot tea-pot with a knitted Christmas-bauble cosy sat at one end, where Jacob's mother now stood.

'Do sit down, everyone—and help yourself.'

Seb tucked in with gusto—which was surprising, considering the size of his breakfast—whereas Jacob took nothing, only accepting a mug of tea. Eva noticed that Jacob's gaze kept flicking to a photograph on the mantelpiece that looked like a picture of him with a blonde woman.

Michelle?

In the picture Jacob sat with his arm around the woman's shoulders as they both posed on what looked like an old country stile. She had long honey-coloured hair, almost down to her waist, and they had their heads together, grinning for the camera.

She had clearly been cherished. And was obviously much remembered, with her picture having pride of place in one of the main rooms of this home.

Eva accepted tea and politely took a biscuit, wondering if the Dolans would ever put *her* picture up? She hoped so. It had started well, so far...

'It's so wonderful to meet you at last, Seb,' Mrs Dolan said. 'Your daddy has told us so much about you. Are you looking forward to Christmas?'

Seb nodded, his mouth full of mince pie.

She smiled broadly. 'We hear you like animals?'

Seb nodded again, stuffing in another mouthful.

'We'll take you out later and show you them all, and then you must visit the orchard. It's where your father used to play.'

Seb looked at his dad and grinned.

Jacob smiled back. 'It's also where I first broke my arm, trying to jump the small stream that's there, so try not to be *too* like me. We don't need to take you to A&E again.'

Mrs Dolan took a biscuit for herself. 'Of course! You had an accident, didn't you? Bumped your head? Were you scared, Seb?'

'A bit...'

Mrs Dolan looked up at her son, then at Eva. 'You're both at the same casualty department, aren't you?'

Eva nodded and smiled. This was so *odd*! They were talking to her as if everything was normal. As if she was *wanted* there. It felt great!

'We've been here in this house forever, it seems. Ever since Jacob was a little boy himself. A bit younger than you, Seb. You must get him to show you the tree where he carved his name.'

'If I can still remember which tree it is.'

'Of *course* you remember. You might not have been here for a while, but you know this place like the back of your hand.'

'You mentioned an orchard, Mrs Dolan? What do you grow there?' Eva ventured her first question, feeling her cheeks flame with heat as everyone turned to face her at the table.

'Bits of everything, really. Apples, pears, greengages, plums—you name it, we've got pies made of it in the freezer! In the spring it looks amazing, when it's all in blossom. And you must call me Molly, dear. Mrs Dolan makes me sound like my mother-in-law!'

Molly Dolan smiled and her whole face creased with delight and happiness.

These people were being *nice* to her! It seemed so strange! It wasn't what she'd been expecting from them at all! A childish delight was filling her on the inside as she soaked up their warmth.

'I'll show you around,' Jacob suggested. 'Fancy a walk? Stretch the legs?'

'Oh, finish your tea first!' Molly urged. 'Always in a rush to get away, Jacob. You've only just got in and sat down.'

'We've been sat down for nearly four hours, Mum. In the car.'

'But Eva needs time to absorb everything. This is all new for her.' She turned to Eva. 'He's always the same when he gets here. It's as if he can't wait to shrug off the city—he has to go out and roam around the place and get the country back into his blood. How he got any work done in Africa, I'll never know.'

She'd mentioned Africa. Jacob's bolthole. But she hadn't mentioned it with any discomfort. She'd not said it as a preamble for launching into a round of questions for her son. She looked as if she was comfortable sitting and waiting until Jacob was ready to talk about it.

Eva sipped her tea. It was perfect. Not too strong. And as she looked across the table at Jacob she began to understand him a bit more. He had a lovely family. Warm, welcoming parents. And he was clearly loved.

Maybe she would be, too?

Eva and Jacob were strolling through the orchard. Seb was with his grandfather, learning the whistles that were used to control the sheepdog, and they could hear them faintly in the distance.

The sun was shining down brightly, but there was no warmth in the cold air and Eva was glad she'd chosen a long coat, hat and scarf. She could feel the sun on her face only barely, and her toes were going numb with cold. It was a strange feeling. But it didn't bother her too much.

She loved the winter. The shortening of the days, getting cosy in front of a fire at night, drinking hot cocoa and being warm and dry inside whilst outside the weather was doing its worst. Wondering when it might snow...

This was the first opportunity she'd had in ages to enjoy the season. She'd been working so much just lately, and had been covering extra shifts until Jacob's arrival. It always got busier towards Christmas in A&E. People and alcohol didn't always mix well, and there was a reason it was called the 'silly season'. There weren't often moments when she could feel carefree and relaxed, and this was a bonus.

All those hours spent worrying in the car... Wasted! She could have sung along to those Christmas songs after all. Mr and Mrs Dolan were lovely. And now she was here, at Jacob's home, with him walking alongside her.

It was hard not to keep stealing glances at him, wondering how he was doing being back here, surrounded by memories. She was enjoying the warmth of his family and feeling she belonged.

'It's very beautiful here, Jacob.'

He nodded and smiled at her. They were walking at a slow pace, with no apparent direction. Just ambling together through the trees.

'You have a wonderful family.' It was true. 'The type I used to dream of having.'

'Thank you.'

She looked directly at him and stopped walking. 'Can I ask something?'

He nodded, squinting at her in the winter sunlight. 'Sure.'

'Why did you have no contact with them? They clearly love you. Care for you. I can understand how you didn't want to be facing old memories by *being* here, but why didn't you keep in contact with them?'

He stopped walking and faced her. They were in a bit of a glade, surrounded by bare, knobbly trees. A robin chirped near them, singing its melody to mark its territory for any other robin that might be listening. It was a happy sound.

He sighed, looking about him. 'It's difficult to say. I know they love me—and please don't think that I take that for granted. I don't. It's just…I knew what it would be like after my wedding day. After Michelle died. They'd look at me with pity, and they'd want to support me and look after me, and I just felt that I didn't deserve it.'

'I don't understand. *Why* didn't you deserve it?'

'It was my fault she died.'

'But you weren't driving that truck that hit her. You couldn't have known that would happen.'

'I know, but…' He trailed off and stuck his hands into his pockets, obviously wrestling with telling her more.

Why wouldn't he say it? Did he not trust her enough yet? Or—her heart sank—perhaps he didn't want to say it because he knew the admission would hurt her.

He still loves Michelle.

'I can't tell you.' He shook his head.

Her worst fears were realised. He still had feelings for his dead fiancée! That *had* to be it. It couldn't be anything else. It was the only thing she could think of that would stop him from confiding in her.

The knowledge of what he was hiding pained her like a punch in the gut. Trying to be brave, trying not to show how much the realisation hurt, she decided to be magnanimous. She would still be his friend, and she was here to help him get through his memories.

'You've made a big step forward by coming here today. You should be proud.' Her voice almost broke as she thought about how she would have to step back from him.

'The place reminds me so much of Michelle…'

As he looked about him Eva tried hard not to show how much his words hurt.

'We played here.' He gestured at the ground. 'Right in this spot. That tree over there… We climbed it. Many times. Tried to build a tree house in it. That small stream… That was where we built the rope swing. And inside the house in every room there's a reminder of her.'

Of course there is! I should never have come today. I could never compete with her memory.

'I saw the picture on the mantel. Is that her?'

He nodded.

'She was very beautiful.'

'She was.'

'What happened to you after she died?'

He let out a big sigh. 'I shut down. I couldn't face any-one. I couldn't bear their sympathy and their pity. I headed up north. Went to Scotland. Somehow managed to find a B & B that had a room and spent the New Year there. Then I just wandered around, basically, though I came back for the funeral.'

She swallowed a painful lump in her throat, realising the depth of his feelings for Michelle. She couldn't com-pete with this kind of love.

'That must have been difficult.'

'It was. I didn't want to see anyone. Didn't want their words of comfort. Michelle was dead because of *me*. Her mother was alone, crying, her heart in pieces, because of *me*.'

'I've told you—it wasn't your fault Michelle's car got hit.'

'Wasn't it?'

His eyes had darkened and the mood had shifted. She could tell he still had a lot of pent-up feelings about what had happened.

'No. It wasn't. Jacob…' She stood in front of him and took his gloved hands in hers. The sun was shining into her eyes and she was having to squint to see, but she could see his tortured face in front of her. 'What happened to Michelle *wasn't* your fault. You've got to let go of that thought. Stop running from it.'

'That's the problem with running. You take your prob-lems with you. They're still in your head.'

'I know. When Seb was born I felt so much guilt. Guilt that he didn't have a father, as I hadn't had a father. Guilt that he didn't have a family around him, the way children should. And even though I did what I could to be a dad as well as a mum, I carried that guilt around with me like a millstone. It's still there. I still feel it even though you're here now. I still worry. What if you leave? What if you're not ready? I've let you in, I've let Seb get to know you and love you, and yet you could still leave. I know what it feels like to lug heavy thoughts around.'

He squeezed her fingers and lifted them to his lips, kissing her hands. 'I won't leave.'

Mesmerised by the action, wanting more than she knew he could give, she looked up into his eyes. 'You won't?'

He shook his head. 'No. I couldn't. Not now.'

'You'll stay for Seb?'

I know he's not staying for me.

He released her hands and stroked her face. 'I'll stay for you both.'

He lowered his head to hers to kiss her, checking her reaction for any sign that she might refuse him—checking that she welcomed his kiss.

Oh, she welcomed it! Wanted it. Wanted *him*! Despite her fears, despite her worries, she embraced the warmth of his soft lips as if it was the last kiss she would ever have from him.

It was bittersweet. Knowing now how he felt about Michelle, she accepted that she would have to take a step back from him. Just let he and Seb be close. There was no room in his heart for *her*, too. Not now. He was a man wrapped up in the past, tethered by his pain to a ghost.

His lips claimed hers, and as his tongue hesitantly entered her mouth and licked her own she almost groaned with wishful yearning and grief for her loss of him.

The orchard was forgotten. Netherfield Village. The house. Jacob's family was forgotten. Here beneath the weak winter sun, in Jacob's arms, was exactly where she should be. But her heart was pained. She knew she couldn't have him. This might be their final kiss. The end of their romance.

'Eva…I'm so glad I met you.'

Eva took a step back—away from his arms, away from what she wanted. Breaking contact, she managed a weak smile. 'I know. Me, too. But…I'm not sure I'm ready for this. And to tell you the truth I'm not sure that *you're* ready for this, either.'

He frowned as the sun shone down on his dark hair, and she couldn't help but notice how delicious he looked in his jeans and boots and a heavy black jacket. Still tanned and healthy from his African adventure.

She sidestepped a snail that had not yet made it into hibernation, unwilling to ruin another life as she moved farther away from Jacob.

'We both made our choices in the past, but it was easier to do so then. It was just us. Me alone. You alone. But now we have Seb, and we have to make the right decisions. The right *choices*. So we'll get it right for *him*.'

He nodded, studying her face, clearly hurt by her words. She watched him look at her, no doubt noticing the smattering of freckles that she could never quite hide with make-up, the way her mouth was curved into a false smile. He'd focused on her lips…

'We should get through Christmas and then…start making some decisions,' she said.

Jacob nodded. 'Okay. I'll ask Dr Clarkson if there's a chance to extend my contract.'

'Right. Okay.'

'And what should we tell Seb? Do we tell him we're together or…? Kids are perceptive. Do we say anything at all?'

She didn't want to tell Seb anything! Why would she risk devastating her son? She would die before she let that happen!

'I think we should keep quiet for a while. We can discuss what's happening later.'

'Later?'

'When you've worked through everything. When you're finally...free.'

He looked at her and slowly nodded. And she knew that he could see she was putting the brakes on their relationship.

Seb was out exploring the farm with Jacob and his dad, and Eva was in the farmhouse kitchen with his mother, helping her to clear up. There was an easy atmosphere between them and they worked well together—Molly wiping down the kitchen surfaces as Eva dried the dishes and put them away.

They'd had a lovely home-made soup for lunch—carrot with coriander that had been grown by the Dolans—accompanied by Molly's rustic bread rolls, filled with sundried tomato and onion seeds, which had taken the simple meal to another level. Now she was sated.

If I were a cat, I'd be curled up in front of the Aga.

Eva put the last of the dishes away, folded the tea towel and stood by the kitchen window. Looking out, she could see Seb and Jacob, chasing each other in the grounds, and she smiled.

Molly came to stand next to her. 'I never thought I'd see the day.'

'Me, neither.'

'Jacob...here...back on the farm. With his family. Where he's meant to be. It's going to make this Christmas really special, having him back.'

Eva glanced at the older woman and saw a sadness in her eyes she'd never noticed before. Was it sadness at not having known about Seb? Was this going to be it? The moment Jacob's parents told her how they really felt about missing out on their grandchild? Was this the point when the nice family turned on her?

'I'm so sorry, Molly.'

'What for, dear?'

'For not persevering in trying to find Jacob—or any of you—to tell you about Seb. If you're mad at me, I'll totally understand—'

Molly turned to look at her in shock. 'We're not *mad* at you! Oh, my dear, we couldn't be happier! All right, we missed out on Seb's early years and we'll never get those back, but you've given us the greatest gift in Seb, and because of him we've got our Jacob back.' She patted Eva's arm. 'Sit with me. I want to tell you something.'

They sat down together at the broad oak table.

'We never thought we'd see Jacob again after what happened—' She stopped short, clearly unsure as to whether to say anything more, glancing over to the picture on the mantel.

'I know about Michelle.'

Molly nodded gratefully. 'I didn't want to say anything unless he'd told you. Michelle was a wonderful girl. She was lovely and she and Jacob made a happy couple. She grew up next door and was always in and out of our house. She never had any siblings, and we used to think she enjoyed all the family chaos she found here. It wasn't till later we realised it was all because of her feelings for Jacob. She seemed so carefree and full of life, and we were all surprised when she became a trainee barrister—it all seemed so very serious for such a sweet girl. When they got engaged our Jacob was head over heels in love. It looked like his life was becoming sorted. A doctor…engaged to be married… The future looked great for them both. When they set a date for the wedding we were all so happy for them. Our son was going to be settled and we wouldn't have to worry about him anymore.'

It was painful to listen to, but Eva could picture it all too well. 'But then she died…'

'Then she died,' Molly repeated, nodding her head softly. 'We were all devastated—most especially her mother. I did what I could to help her through it, but Jacob just disappeared. We were *so* worried. Frantic! We didn't know where he'd gone.'

'Grief does strange things to people.'

Her eyes went dark. 'It does. I've seen it. I never thought we'd get back the Jacob that we know and love so much, but here he is, with a son of his own, and he's smiling again. We have *you* to thank for that, Eva. We can never thank you enough.'

Molly took Eva's hands in her own and held them tightly, squeezing hard.

Eva smiled back, and then gave Molly a hug. Was this what it was like to be hugged by a mum? It felt so good, and Molly was so soft and warm and welcoming. A part of her didn't want to let Molly go!

Tears painfully pricked her eyes at this feeling of being so near, yet so far. Of almost having become a part of the only family that had ever welcomed her.

The next day they all sat down to a hearty breakfast together, though Eva didn't eat much after a sleepless night. Molly stood over the cooker, making a full English breakfast, wearing a flowery apron and beaming at them all like the cat that had got the cream.

Eva could see why she was so happy. She not only had her son back within the fold of her family, but a new grandson, too.

Jacob suggested they might go for a walk into the village and have a look around before lunch.

Molly thought that was a great idea. 'We'll come, too! We could have lunch at The Three Horseshoes before you have to go home.'

They all set off, wrapped up in their winter coats, with Seb splashing through ice-covered puddles and making a nice muddy mess of his trousers.

As they got closer to the village of Netherfield, Seb began to complain that his legs were getting tired.

'Come here, champ.' Jacob lifted him up into the air and over his shoulders for a shoulder ride.

'Watch your jacket!' Eva warned, noting the muddy rivulets running down Seb's boots.

'That doesn't matter. The jacket will wash.' He held on to Seb's hands and they walked ahead of the others, Seb giggling happily, perched up high.

Molly fell into step beside Eva and threaded her arm through hers. 'Don't they make a wonderful sight, the two of them?'

She smiled. 'They do.'

'You must be so happy they're getting on well?' Molly asked.

Eva nodded, forcing a smile. 'Oh, I am! Christmas is going to be so special this year for Seb.'

'And for Jacob, too, I suspect. He deserves a happy Christmas again. Things are looking up at last for the Dolans!'

Eva said nothing. Were things looking up for *her*, too?

Jacob stood with his father at the bar of The Three Horseshoes. They'd given their group's food order and were waiting for their drinks to be served so they could take the tray to their table.

His dad patted him on the back. 'It's good to have you back, son. We've missed you.'

Jacob smiled. 'I'm sorry I went AWOL for so long, Dad. It wasn't fair on you and Mum.'

'We understood. We know you felt guilty about Michelle, but so did everyone else. You felt guilty... We felt guilty...'

'Why did *you* feel guilty?'

'Because we couldn't protect you from the pain you were in.'

Jacob could feel his eyes welling up. The burn of tears was being held back from bursting forth by sheer will. He was suddenly overwhelmed. Glad to have come home. Glad to be back with family and glad that they understood him.

Eva had been right from the beginning. About him coming back. She'd known more about family than he had.

He turned and looked at her across the pub. She sat with his mother, was smiling at something Seb was saying. But he could see that she was holding back. She had been ever since that moment in the orchard. They'd kissed and then... something had happened. She'd created distance between them and now she seemed to be...apart from them all.

It was probably for the best, even if he didn't like it. He couldn't be with Eva the way he wanted to be unless he told her the whole truth of what had happened. That was the only way he could fully give her his heart. By being honest. But if he *did* tell her... His heart sank at the thought. She would turn away from him. She would be appalled at what he'd done. She would want nothing to do with him and he couldn't risk that.

But she's already turning away from me and I don't want to lose her!

Their gazes met across the bar. Eva looked at him for a moment and then glanced away.

And he knew, in that moment, that he was already losing her.

CHAPTER SEVEN

LEAVING NETHERFIELD HAD almost made her cry. For the first time in her life she had felt welcomed by another family. Jacob's parents had managed to put right, in a single weekend, the years of hurt and pain she had felt every time she'd been sent back to the children's home. She could remember every occasion of being placed in the back of the car, solemnly refusing to turn back and wave at the family she was leaving.

But that Sunday as they'd left Jacob's parents she *had* turned round. She'd waved, she'd fought back tears, and she'd felt as if she was waving goodbye to them forever.

Being in Jacob's company was becoming more difficult. She *wanted* to be with him! Had developed feelings for him. Wanted to connect with him, physically and emotionally. But she knew she had to hold herself back until his feelings for his dead fiancée had been resolved.

If that were possible.

She'd died in such tragic circumstances…Jacob would probably always feel *something* for her.

Her yearning for him was intense. It was as if her body *craved* him when he was near. She would breathe more heavily, she would tighten her hands into fists to stop herself from reaching out to touch him, she would lick her lips in memory of his sweet kisses…

It was torture…

She felt scared. She'd never wanted a man so much! Never wanted to be with his family so much! To turn up again at Netherfield and know she'd be welcomed. That people would smile and be overjoyed at her arrival.

Eva had never had that before. And she wanted it back. Not just for her, but for Seb, too. For all this time they'd been alone, never knowing what they were missing out on, but now they could be a part of that. A part of his family.

But how much of a part? Even Molly had asked what was going on between her and Jacob.

She knew what she would *like* to be going on. But he wasn't ready. Jacob had shared things with her. Personal things. Thoughts. Emotions. The events of his past, as she had with him. But there was still the ghost of Michelle.

Did Michelle rule Jacob's heart? Would he ever let her go? Was he holding himself back from her because deep down he still loved Michelle?

Was she trying to compete with a ghost?

Because that wasn't a battle that anyone could win.

Jacob was generally happy with the way the visit to his parents' place had gone. He'd really not known how his parents would react. He'd expected his mum to go over the top, to cry a bit, maybe gush about having him back and ask him to promise never to go away again.

But she hadn't. She'd been just fine. Dad, too. They'd been thrilled to have him back, but they'd made the weekend more about Seb—about welcoming him and his mother into the family and making them feel comfortable.

He'd observed, as if from a distance. Letting it all be about them unless his mother had particularly asked his opinion on something or deliberately involved him. It had been so good to be back. He hadn't been overwhelmed by memories, as he'd expected himself to be. It had been bearable.

Because of Eva and Seb.

If it hadn't have been for them he knew he would never have managed the weekend without feeling haunted. But their being there had somehow stopped all of that.

Because of them the visit had been about the future. About how much Seb and Eva could be involved. About how much they were now a *family*.

Of course his mum had fed them all as if they'd never seen food before, and had insisted on packing them off for the journey home with freezer bags full of sausage rolls and pastries and pies.

They'd stood in the doorway and waved him off with tears in their eyes. Eva had looked tearful, too, but she hadn't wanted to talk about it.

He'd promised his parents he would call within a couple of days.

And he had.

They adored Seb, as he had known they would, but they also adored Eva, and that meant a lot to him.

Eva meant a lot to him. Finding her again had turned his life around. He'd known that first night at the party that she was something special, but to have thought that she would bring him this much happiness… He'd not expected that to happen.

He'd hoped that when he found her again she would be his friend, but other things were happening. As he got to know Seb more, and the more time he spent in their home, the more he was getting to know Eva, and he knew she was more special than he'd ever believed. Could feel it in his heart.

He so wanted to be able to tell her the truth. The *real* truth about what had happened on his wedding day and not the sanitised version that everyone else *thought* was the truth.

But how would she react? That was his biggest concern right now. If he told her before Christmas… But he so wanted to spend this precious time with them—he couldn't tell her!

She would view him with horror. Look at him differently. Judge him. And he couldn't bear the idea of not being with Seb over Christmas. It was just a week away—he could keep it inside until after the Yuletide season, couldn't he?

I should have been honest with her from the start. But how exactly do you say that to someone? That you are responsible for someone's death? It's not the kind of thing you drop into conversation with someone new.

And now that he hadn't told her the truth for so long… it would be harder to say anything at all.

He wanted to be with Eva. He wanted to be with her in a *relationship*.

But he knew that if he unburdened himself of his guilt, she might walk away…

Eva had had enough pain in her past. Did he want to cause her more?

Their days at work began to pass quickly. With Christmas-party season in full swing the doctors were rushed off their feet, dealing with what felt like a swarm of drunk and disorderlies they had to keep an eye on, as well as dealing with all the usual illnesses and injuries.

There was a slew of norovirus lockdowns on various wards, so they had to limit who they admitted into hospital and where they sent them, causing the corridors to be filled with patients on trollies, moaning and groaning to their paramedics that they hadn't been seen yet.

It was a heady mix of patients filled with Christmas cheer and patients who were grumpy and angry. Everyone's temper was getting shorter and shorter.

In the evenings Jacob would come round to Eva's to read to Seb, and Eva would cook them all a meal that they would eat together. It all appeared quite domesticated and happy, but there was a palpable tension that they could both feel, and both of them refused to mention it in their fear of ruining Christmas.

At work, it was getting harder and harder for Eva to be normal around him. Their relationship—whatever it was—was confusing. Jacob was being polite, keeping his distance, and she was feeling hurt by it. She sneaked looks at him when she thought he wasn't watching, and yearned for his touch.

But she knew they had to be absolute professionals, who showed no familiarity, no favouritism, who showed no attraction to each other, and this just further reinforced to Eva the wisdom of his pushing her away.

She knew it was for the best.

But that didn't make it any easier when all she truly wanted was to be in his arms.

One night they were both tidying up in the kitchen after their meal.

Eva was loading the dishwasher and Jacob was passing her the dishes after scraping them clean over the bin. Their fingers kept touching as they passed and accepted plates and other items, and tiny frissons would ripple up her arms each time. She tried to ignore them. Tried to tell herself that she *could not* have this man. Not right now. Not whilst his feelings were so confused.

Politely, she thanked him for each item, and then, when it seemed she was saying 'thank you' too much, she just looked at him and smiled a thank-you. But then he'd smile back, and then those smiles and glances became longer and longer, until they were just standing over the open dishwasher, both holding the same plate and just looking at each other.

The way Jacob was looking at her—as if he was hungry for her, as if he wouldn't be able to breathe unless he kissed her—made her feel all giddy inside. How long had it been since that kiss in the orchard? Not long at all. And yet it felt as if decades had passed.

Her lips parted and she looked at him, desperate to tell him how she felt about him.

Suddenly Jacob stepped around the open dishwasher and kicked the door closed with his foot. He grabbed her and pulled her into his arms.

Eva was backed against one of the kitchen units, could feel the edge of the work surface digging into her bottom as Jacob's body pressed up against hers. She could feel *him*. Every wonderful inch of him. He cupped her face in his hands and tilted her lips up to his. Kissing her, devouring her face with the force of his passion.

Oh, yes!

Kissing him felt so good! As if they were meant to be! His soft lips, his stubble gave her a sweet, yet burning sensation that flowed from her lips down through her body and ignited a fire deep within her that made her crave more of him. More than just a kiss. More than just lips touching.

She wanted everything about him. His hands, his mouth, his *body*. She wanted all of him. To be with him the way they had been when they'd conceived Seb. Naked and entwined. Unable to get enough of each other.

As their kiss deepened her hands found their way under his shirt, feeling the burning heat in his skin, the power-

ful muscles contained within him moving smoothly as he
kissed her.

I want you!

She wanted to say it. She wanted to take that step and
just *tell* him. That she was here. In his present. A real
woman who loved him. Yes, *loved* him—if only he would
give her the chance.

Remember he's in love with someone else.

Eva pushed him away and was left gasping from the
force of his passion.

He looked confused. Hurt. But then his glazed eyes finally got some sense back in them and he stepped away,
out of the kitchen.

She heard the front door open and close with such fi-
nality that she couldn't stop the tears. She cried. Cried for
the fact that she would never have him the way she wanted
to. That until he got over Michelle he would never be hers.

I should have kept him at arm's length. It's too painful.

'He's in cardiac arrest!'

Jacob's patient lay prone on the bed, his eyes closed,
his mouth agape. Greg Harper had been brought in by his
wife, Ginny. He'd been feeling unwell all day, and after an
hour of trying to work the ground in his frost-hardened al-
lotment had come in complaining of being short of breath.
Ginny had said that he'd looked extremely pale and had
felt clammy. She'd called for an ambulance as her senses
had told her it was something serious.

It had been a good decision. Because now Greg was in
a hospital setting as his cardiac arrest occurred, and there-
fore theoretically stood a much higher chance of survival.

Jacob lowered the head of the bed and called for the
crash team. This was his first case of leading a resuscitation since he'd joined the department a few weeks ago.

Eva came running over, along with two other doctors and nurses.

'Compressions!' Jacob requested, his voice stern and clear.

Eva stepped forward to do them, clasping one hand above the other and placing them centrally to Greg's chest. She began to compress his chest, maintaining a steady rhythm, as Jacob called out further orders to the rest of the team.

'I want pads on, and venous access. Sarah—you take the airway and get an oropharyngeal airway in.'

Jacob took a step back and oversaw it all. He stood in front of Ginny, who had hidden behind him, not daring to look.

The defibrillator pads were soon attached to Greg's chest and Eva stopped compressions momentarily for the machine to assess Greg's heart rhythm—if any.

'He's in VF. Shocking.'

The doctor in charge of the machine checked to make sure no one was touching the patient and then pressed the button with the little lightning rod on it. Greg's body juddered slightly.

'He's still in VF.' Sarah looked up at him.

Jacob stood firm. 'Continue CPR. Adrenaline.'

The drug was administered into a vein and Eva continued pumping the chest. Her red hair swung back and forth with the force of her compressions and her breathing was becoming heavier. Compressions could be exhausting—especially if resuscitation took a long time—so they liked to rotate staff every two minutes.

'Please don't let him die! Please save him!' pleaded his wife, Ginny.

'Pulse check, please.'

A nurse checked the radial pulse. 'Weak.'

'Continue.'

Jacob's voice rang loud and clear in the department. Cardiac arrests were dramatic, especially to an onlooker, like a family member or friend, but to a doctor they were some of the easiest cases to deal with in A&E, because there was a recognised pattern of treatment. You knew exactly what you had to do and when you had to do it.

Not every case in the department was so clear-cut. People came in with mystery ailments all the time, or didn't tell the doctors all their symptoms, or lied. Cardiac arrests were obvious and they knew how to deal with them.

'Assess rhythm.'

A further shock was given, then oxygen pumped in via a bag valve and mask.

Jacob glanced at the clock. 'Amiodarone. Three hundred milligrams.'

Greg groaned and his wife gasped, peering round Jacob to see if her husband was showing any signs of waking up.

'Pulse check?'

The nurse felt the patient's wrist. 'I have a strong pulse.'

Sarah, managing the airway and monitoring the machines, confirmed that the patient was making respiratory effort and that blood pressure was slowly rising.

'Well done, team. Once Mr Harper is stable I want him transferred to ITU. Until then I want him on fifteen-minute obs.' Jacob turned to Ginny. 'We've got him back, but we need to make sure we keep him with us. He's in for a difficult twenty-four hours.'

Ginny nodded. 'Yes. Can I speak to him?'

He nodded. 'Of course.'

'Thank you, Doctor! If I'd lost him...'

'You didn't.'

She looked shocked at his abrupt tone, then said firmly, 'He's my *life*.'

The look in her eyes softened his mood and Jacob understood. He laid a hand on her arm apologetically. 'I know. Talk to him. Sit with him. When he gets a bed in ITU I'll come and let you know.'

Ginny smiled her thanks.

He turned at the doorway and looked at her, sitting beside her husband's bed. They were lucky. They'd had each other for years, it seemed. The love. The comfort. Why could *he* not have that? Didn't he deserve it?

What he felt for Eva... He'd allowed his physical desires to overwhelm him the other night. He hadn't been able to help it. She was just so beautiful, and the way they were both holding back had been killing him.

I need to tell her the truth.

No one knew the real truth. Except him and Michelle.

Could he wait until after Christmas? He wanted to. Knew it was probably the best thing. But it was so hard! He loved her and he couldn't have her. Not until she knew the truth—only then could they be together.

If she isn't scared away.

And Eva didn't come alone. She came as a package. With Seb.

He couldn't hurt that boy.

That boy was his life now. If she took him away from him... No. No, she wouldn't do that to him.

Then, what have I got to lose?

Those first nights under the vast African sky he'd thought about Michelle and the way he'd treated her. What he'd done to drive her into the arms of another. He hadn't been able to bear to admit the truth. And his thoughts had always come back to Eva. The woman who had briefly brought him back to life. Thoughts of her had pervaded his mind, but he'd tried to dismiss them as the thoughts of a mixed up, grieving man.

Those nights alone in Africa had made Jacob re-evaluate his life. Think about what he wanted. Not only what he could do for others, but what he needed to do for himself. And all he'd been able to think about was his own family, back on the farm, and the woman with red hair...

Eva.

She'd done a great job with Seb. And all alone, too. She was a strong woman. He had to believe that her internal strength would help get them all through this.

He needed her.

Knew it as he knew the sun would rise in the east.

He burned for her. Couldn't think straight around her anymore.

I should just be honest with her. Get it over with. Then we can move forward. Together.

Jacob spotted Eva across the department. As always, she looked gorgeous. Her curtain of red hair fell in a perfect wave and her crystal-blue eyes looked up at him in question as he walked across to her. She'd made a small nod to the season and was wearing tiny dangling Christmas trees in her ears. They might have looked ridiculous on anyone else, but not her.

He stood in front of her. 'Hi.'

'Hello.'

His fingers itched to touch her. To hold her. Since that kiss in the kitchen it had been killing him to keep himself from touching her. From being with her. How he'd managed to walk away from the house the other night he'd never know.

Her reaction to that last kiss the other night hadn't lied. She'd wanted it, and had responded to it in a way that he'd liked. As his lips had trailed over the delicate skin at her neck he'd inhaled her scent and had almost drifted away on a cloud of ecstasy. She'd smelled so good and she'd felt so right and he'd wanted her again.

He could see no reason to keep punishing himself by staying away. Didn't they both deserve more?

'Eva? May I have a word with you?' His voice was thick and gravelly, as if he was finding it difficult to talk.

'What's up?'

'In private.' He made eye contact and enforced it, staring hard at her, making sure she understood him.

But she seemed nervous. 'Talk to me here.'

She stood up and put her hands into the pockets of the long cardigan she wore.

'Well?'

She was looking up at him, and he so wanted to cup her face and bring those sensuous lips to his own, but he controlled himself and took a step back. 'I need to speak with you.'

'You are.'

'Privately. I thought tonight, when I come round, I could cook *you* dinner for a change.'

'Oh. Okay. That would be nice.'

'I need to tell you *everything*.'

She swallowed. 'Everything?'

He nodded. 'You need to hear it all.'

Eva watched him walk away from her.

He was going to tell her tonight. Tell her that he could not give her his heart. Not until he was over his grieving. He would tell her that he would still like to be there for Seb, but that whatever had been happening between the two of them had to be over.

She bit her lip as she felt tears threaten, but then pushed away her grief.

She wouldn't cry over him anymore.

She would get through tonight and she would be strong. For Seb.

This didn't have to ruin his Christmas. It was only a couple of days away.

Eva set her mind on being strong. On keeping a safe distance. On remaining upbeat.

At least she tried.

Eva came home from her long day at work to gentle piano music on the stereo system, fairy lights and candles lit throughout and the most delicious smells emanating from her kitchen.

She hung up her bag and her jacket and kicked off her shoes, padded barefoot into the lounge. There was no one there so she headed into the kitchen, where Jacob stood stirring something on the hob.

'Where's Seb?'

'With Letty. And she said he could sleep over, too.'

Eva raised an eyebrow. Really? He'd sent Seb on a sleepover? Just how upset did Jacob expect her to be?

He passed her a glass of white wine. Whatever he was cooking smelled mouth-wateringly good. Like Jacob himself.

Stop it!

But it was true. Jacob had a wonderful scent, and when she was up close to him and he held her in his arms...

Eva shook her head to clear it. She needed to think straight. But the idea that there was wine, good food and Jacob... It was all muddying the waters!

Only a few weeks ago life had seemed simple. It had been her and Seb against the world. Then Jacob had come back. And since he'd found out he was a father he'd practically moved in and turned her world upside down! She wasn't even sure she was the same person anymore. She knew she'd changed.

Jacob looked particularly delightful this evening. He wore dark trousers and a crisp white shirt, and his tousled dark hair just crept over the edge of the collar. He had broad, powerful shoulders and a neat waist, and she could only try to remember the powerful, muscular legs beneath the cloth…

He was a sight for sore, tired eyes.

And she wanted him.

The knowledge that he also wanted her, that he'd got himself hot because of her, had barely contained himself because of her, was an aphrodisiac she tried to ignore!

'What's cooking?'

Jacob turned, and the beam of his smile lighting up his face brightened her heart. He was trying to put things right. He was trying to give her a good night before he ruined it with whatever news he thought he still had to share.

'An African specialty. Yam and crayfish risotto, inspired by my time in Gabon, followed by a *malva* pudding.'

'What's a *malva* pudding?'

He smiled. 'It's very rich, very buttery, and filled to the brim with syrup. You'll love it.'

She nodded. Sounded good. 'Wow. You really did learn a lot in Africa. When did you go to Gabon?'

'In between my times at the clinic.'

'And what did you discover?'

Her mouth dried as Jacob took a few steps towards her. He was literally millimetres away from her, towering above her and staring down into her eyes as if he'd just discovered the most beautiful jewel in existence and was hypnotised by it.

'I discovered that I'd left behind the one person who could've changed my life.'

Her. He meant *her*.

And, boy, was that electrifying stuff! She felt so alive with him standing right there, looking down at her, devouring her with his gaze. She felt as if she was waiting for him to inch those last few millimetres closer, so that her body could lock into his, like a key in a padlock.

Were they made for each other? She felt that it might be that way. Physically anyway. But what about the other stuff? The boring stuff that grown-ups had to think about. Like trust and reliability and dependability. And love.

Did Jacob love her? She knew he loved Seb. He was definitely there for his son, and it seemed he spent every spare moment he had at her house. But what of his feelings for *her*? There was a definite attraction between them, but was he still in love with his dead fiancée?

'Jacob, I don't know what I am to you.'

He tilted his head, as if questioning her. 'You're very important to me.'

'Important? Is that all?'

Jacob looked shocked and upset. 'You're Seb's mum. You're the woman I can't stop thinking about. You chase every other thought out of my head and, believe me, that's difficult to do.'

She put her wine glass down and turned to face him. '*Every* other thought?'

He smiled. 'Most of them.'

'It's the ones you don't tell me about that worry me.'

'I *will* tell you. But I'd like us to enjoy our evening first. Let's allow ourselves that. Forget the difficulties for a moment. Just enjoy being with each other for now.'

She could do that. She didn't like postponing the pain that she knew was coming, but she wanted to enjoy him whilst she could. If pain was coming, then so be it, but there was no reason why she couldn't just let go and enjoy being with the man she loved for a few moments more.

She smiled. 'So what do we do now?'

Jacob smiled back at her. 'Eat dinner. Start afresh. Can you do that with me?'

Maybe. It was scary still.

But perhaps I'm tired of being alone?

She stood up and grabbed her wine glass. 'Let's eat dinner.'

Jacob nodded, smiling.

The crayfish and yam risotto was divine! The yam was sweet and soft and the crayfish was succulent and melted in her mouth.

Eva glanced at Jacob. 'This is lovely, by the way. You might not have noticed from the way I've gobbled it all up like a hippo.'

Jacob picked his fork up and grinned. 'I had noticed, and I didn't for one minute compare you to a hippo. And thank you. It's a compliment.'

She took another mouthful, and when she'd swallowed it she looked at him across the table. 'Tell me more about Africa. Your work there.'

He met her gaze and nodded slightly, his face thoughtful. 'Well, you know about Reuben. But there were so many people out there who all changed my life in a small way.'

'I'd like to hear about it.'

'Cataract surgery was the first thing I did. There just seemed to be a never-ending line of people with the need for eye surgery. Not just old people, but kids, too. Seeing a child regain his eyesight was amazing, each and every time.'

'I can imagine.'

'There was this one kid who saw his mum for the first time when he was eight years old. The look of happiness on his face afterwards...' Jacob had a faraway look in his eyes and simply smiled.

Eva could only imagine how he must have felt. 'You said you helped build a school?'

'That was much later—but, yes. Again, there were just so many kids who'd never even seen inside a classroom and we could quickly build one in about a week. To see them all go in and meet their teacher, start writing on blackboards... It made me appreciate all that I'd had in my life. All that I'd taken for granted.'

'Sometimes we need reminding.'

'With each patient I met, each story I heard, it just made me realise that I was getting ready to come home. To find *my* happiness again. To believe that I could have it.'

Eva nodded.

'The African people are so noble. And proud. But in a good way. They're honest and heartfelt...and even though most of them hardly have any material things they're intensely happy if they have family.'

'Did you feel alone out there?'

'To begin with. But I ignored it. I've always been headstrong, but being in Africa taught me that sometimes you need to pause and reflect. Think things through.'

'Before you came back?'

He nodded, intense blue eyes staring back at her from across the table.

'And what do you want from life now?' Her breath hitched in her throat as she half hoped he'd say her, but she was half afraid he'd say something else.

'You. And Seb. I came back intent on finding you and I did. I'm going to be really honest now and say it—and hope

I don't sound like some kind of mad stalker. It was no accident that I walked into your A&E. I knew you were there.'

She gasped. Shocked. He'd *known*? Then that meant he'd known exactly where he would find her when he came back! He'd pretended it was a surprise to walk in and find her!

'But you had no idea about what happened after you left. About Seb.'

'No. And once I was over the shock it was a wonderful surprise. Regret, yes, for the lost years...' Eva's eyes were downcast, so he reached out and grasped her hand with his own. 'But joy at having more family. An amazing son with the woman that I...'

She looked up. 'Yes?'

What would he say? That he loved her? She almost couldn't breathe, waiting for him to say it.

He stared at her intently. 'That I have feelings for.'

Eva exhaled. Slowly.

'Feelings? What kind of feelings?' She licked her lips, watching as his eyes tracked the movement, then moved back up to look into her eyes.

'Strong feelings. I want us to try to be together. Properly.' He stood up from his side of the table and came round to hers.

She watched him move, aware that her heart was pounding and her breathing was getting heavier, her mouth drying in anticipation. 'Jacob—'

He took her hand in his and bade her rise from her seat. 'Would you come with me?'

'Where?' she croaked, her voice almost not working at all.

'Upstairs.'

Upstairs. To bed. Sex. That was what he meant.

She wanted to. Physically, her body wanted that very much, as did her heart, but her head was telling her to think twice. Tomorrow was Christmas Eve. The anniversary of his wife-to-be's death. The anniversary of the night they'd slept together for the first time. Did she want to sleep with him knowing that he didn't feel for her the way she felt about him?

She shook her head. 'I can't be anyone's second best, Jacob.'

He stroked her face. 'You could never be second best for me.'

Jacob gazed down at her, his eyes glazed with a sexual hunger that she wanted to satisfy. Feelings be damned! Why *shouldn't* she have him? The last time she'd slept with him had been all those years ago, and though the memories of that night were awe-inspiring, she wanted to be with him one last time—no matter what happened afterwards.

Jacob scooped her up into his arms and carried her easily up the stairs and into her bedroom, closing the door softly behind them.

Eva, laughing, allowed Jacob to set her down on the edge of the bed. She looked at him, watching as he stood before her, undoing the buttons of his shirt from top to bottom.

It was mesmerising.

He pulled his shirt from his trousers, and as soon as she saw the smattering of dark hair that dipped beneath his belt buckle she quickly stood up, unable to stay away from him a moment longer, and helped him off with his clothes.

To have him before her, totally naked, as she slowly slipped off her own clothes, was magical. The memory she had of him, of a younger, less muscular Jacob, was stunning enough, but to see him now—more heavily set, broader, stronger—was a powerful aphrodisiac.

And he wanted *her*.

Eva slowly reached out to touch him. Her doubts silenced.

* * *

Eva blinked and opened her eyes. Frosty sunlight was streaming in through the open curtains at her bedroom window and her body felt deliciously exhausted.

Christmas Eve!

What time was it?

She felt as if something had woken her, but she couldn't think what. Had there been a sound? Her alarm clock?

Blinking, she turned and glanced at it. Ten minutes past seven. Still early. Yawning, she turned back to look at Jacob, asleep in the bed beside her. His dark hair was all tousled and wavy. From sleep? Or from her fingers? It could easily be both. There'd been moments last night when she'd held his head in her hands as his tongue had worked its magic and she'd grabbed hold of him, her fingers splaying in his hair as he'd brought her to ecstasy.

What a night!

His face looked so relaxed this morning, and he had a five-o'clock shadow darkening his jaw. She'd felt that stubble last night and it had been delicious, tickling her skin and her tender places. Her inner thighs felt roughened and sore. But in a good way.

He was lying on his stomach, his head resting on his hands, and he looked so peaceful, his suntanned skin set healthily against the white of her sheets. His muscled arms and powerful shoulders a delightful addition to her bedroom. And farther beneath the sheets... *Oh, my!*

Last night had been even better than the night she'd spent with him four years ago. She wanted to reach out and touch him just once more, to prove that this was real. As she did so, and her fingers touched his jawline, his eyes opened and he smiled slowly.

'Morning.'

'Good morning.'

He was blinking at the half-light coming through the bedroom curtains. 'The night got away from us.'

'It did.' Swinging her legs out of bed, she grabbed her robe.

'Where are you going?'

'To make some tea. Want one?'

He pulled himself into an upright position, the sheets just barely covering his modesty. 'Sounds great.'

Smiling, she headed downstairs and into her kitchen. The remains of their meal last night were still there, and she smiled at the memory of the food and what had come after...

Then her thoughts darkened. They hadn't talked. They hadn't discussed what they'd meant to. Should she raise it now? Was this a good time to remind him of her doubts?

Look at what had happened last night! It had been amazing! Skin tingling, electrifying. The passion that had been between them...

That's how it could be between us if we let it. If we refuse to face what we don't want to face.

She wasn't sure if they could do that. Surely the lies they were telling themselves would soon creep to the surface and ruin what they had?

No. They *had* to talk. It was the only way.

She couldn't quite believe it. Everything was going right in her world. She'd gained the family she'd always dreamed of. They could be a unit. They were both striving for the same goals. They were both there for Seb.

They were there for each other.

Mostly.

She laid her hand on her heart as she looked out of the kitchen window, waiting for the kettle to boil. She could feel it beating. *Dum-dum. Dum-dum.* It didn't have to beat alone anymore. She'd lain her head on Jacob's chest last night as they'd fallen asleep together and it had beat with the same rhythm. *Dum-dum. Dum-dum.*

She was no longer alone!

Eva wasn't sure what she'd done to deserve so much happiness. Perhaps after all her years of suffering as a child, of being alone, being the outsider, this was her reward now? This sense of belonging that she felt being with both Seb *and* Jacob?

Whatever it was, it was amazing.

She made the tea, and some toast, and prepared a tray to take upstairs. For the first time in her life she would have breakfast in bed, and then *she* would be the one to cause her life to come crashing down around her ears.

She'd let him have a shower. Then she'd had one and now they were both dressed.

As he pushed his belt into its buckle, he looked at her. 'What's wrong?'

She looked up at him from her seat on the bed, nerves racing through her body, causing her heart to pound like a jackhammer as the possibility of abandonment crept ever nearer.

'We never did talk last night.'

His eyes darkened. 'No, we didn't.'

'I think we ought to.'

Jacob stared at her. 'But last night… We…we were so good together! I'm not sure I want to taint that with what I have to say.'

Eva wrapped her cardigan tightly around herself. Neither was she. But she couldn't move forward in a relationship with him if she was lying to herself and allowing him to lie to her.

'Nor do I. But I think we both need to be truthful. For Seb as much as for ourselves.'

He sighed and settled down on the bed across from her. 'You're right.'

She sucked in a breath. Okay. She was ready.

'Tell me.'

He nodded, thinking, his eyes downcast. Then he looked up at her.

'On my wedding day something happened that...that no one knows about.'

Okay. That wasn't the direction she'd thought this would start, but she'd go with it.

'What?'

'Michelle made it to the church. She didn't die on her way to the service like I told everyone. She made it there.'

Eva was confused. 'She *made* it?'

'Remember I told you that I was outside, waiting for the first glimpse of the wedding car? I'd been too fidgety inside, so I was walking around to rid myself of the nerves. Then suddenly she pulled up in her car.'

'You *saw* her?'

He nodded. 'She wanted to speak to me before the service. She told me that she'd cheated on me. With my best friend Marcus. She said that I hadn't loved her the way I ought to and so she'd looked elsewhere.'

Eva hadn't expected this! 'She *cheated* on you?'

'She said she still loved me, that she wanted to go on with the wedding but wanted to enter our marriage honestly.'

He paused for a moment, then stood and began to pace the room.

'I was furious! Furious that she'd cheated on me, but furious with myself, too—because I'd *known* something wasn't right and I'd ignored it. I knew there was no way I could marry her still. We argued. I said some things...*horrible* things. I don't know what came over me, but I ripped into her verbally. I couldn't bear to look at her. The more I looked at her, the more I hated her. I ordered her to go away. Told her I never wanted to see her again for as long as I lived. She was crying, mascara all over the place, begging for my forgiveness, but I told her to—'

'What?'

'Something *horrible*. She ran from me. Ran back to her car and screeched off. I knew she was driving recklessly, but I was so angry I didn't care!'

Eva covered her mouth with her hand. They'd argued and then she'd died? No wonder he felt awful!

'Jacob…'

'I stood outside the church for ages. Trying to think of how I was going to go inside and face everyone. Tell them the wedding was off.'

'So what happened then?'

'The police arrived.'

She knew what was coming.

'They said that Michelle had died. That she'd been in a car crash, had been thrown from the vehicle. Everyone assumed that she'd died on her way to the church. They were all crying and weeping and dabbing at their eyes with tissues and I just couldn't bear it! It was all so false! None of them knew the truth and all of them wanted to pity me. Wanted to see me collapse in a heap of tears.'

'You must have been in shock.'

'I didn't know *what* to feel. I'd been furious with her and sent her away and she'd got killed. *My* fault. If I hadn't sent her away… If I'd given us a chance…'

Eva couldn't believe it! She could see now how difficult that must have been. For him to have known the truth— that Michelle had cheated—and yet for absolutely everyone else to think they'd been so in love. As she had. But if this was what he'd been hiding, then perhaps he *wasn't* still in love with Michelle!

'*This* is what you've been keeping from me?'

He stood in front of her. 'I'll understand if you don't want anything to do with me,' he said.

She stared at his face. At the pain in his eyes. Seeing the way he was so bowed down by the guilt he'd been carrying all these years.

She was about to say something when there was a furious banging on her front door.

'Eva! *Eva?* It's Letty! Hurry—it's Seb!'

Letty…? Seb…?

She flew down the stairs, Jacob following close behind, watching helplessly as she fumbled over her keys to unlock the front door. Then she flung the door wide.

Letty stood there, with Seb draped in her arms, pale and unconscious.

'Oh, my God!'

'I can't wake him!'

Eva stared at her almost lifeless son and felt her legs give way.

'*Seb?*' She shook his shoulders gently, then with more force. When he didn't respond she pinched his earlobe. Nothing. She placed her ear over his mouth.

He was still breathing!

The doctor inside her started to analyse, and her gut filled with a nasty sensation as she just knew that something bad had happened.

'Call an ambulance.' She turned to Jacob, but he was already on his mobile.

This was wrong. So very badly wrong.

She kept trying to rouse her son as Jacob spoke on the phone to ambulance control.

'He won't wake up. Not responding to voice commands. Not responding to pain. He's unconscious.'

Eva looked up at him. 'Wouldn't it be quicker to drive him in ourselves?'

'In rush hour? No. Let's wait for the ambulance.'

It was agonising just to sit and wait. To know what they knew and think of all the horrible things it might be. Meningitis? Encephalitis? An infection? Something caused by the earlier accident?

It took an age, it seemed, before the ambulance arrived outside her house.

The paramedics, at least, were familiar to her. Friendly faces. People she trusted. Letty quickly relayed how she'd found him that morning and told them that he'd seemed okay the night before, except for saying he had a headache.

'What?' Eva frowned. 'He had a headache? Why didn't you tell me?'

Letty looked upset. 'I'm so sorry. I didn't think it was that bad.'

The headache could be vital. Different diagnoses flashed through her mind…all the things it could be. But her brain kept telling her just one thing.

Meningitis.

She knew it in her heart, but didn't want to admit it. Not Seb. Not her boy. *No.* It was Christmas. This couldn't be happening at *Christmas.* It was wrong. He shouldn't be like this. He should be getting excited about presents under the tree and Christmas carolling, or looking out for snow…

The paramedics quickly gave him oxygen and bundled him into the ambulance in double-quick time. They allowed Eva in, but held their hands up at Jacob.

'Sorry—only room for one. Can you get to the hospital under your own steam?' And they set off with lights and siren going.

Eva sat in the back with her son, reeling as they went around corners and bollards and through traffic lights, knowing that Jacob would be trying to travel separately behind them in his own car. But he wouldn't be allowed to speed, or to go on the wrong side of the road, and would be delayed in getting to the hospital by traffic lights that they could just speed through.

Briefly she thought about what he'd just told her. About his wedding day. About what had really happened with Michelle. But she pushed it away. That didn't matter now! She needed to focus on Seb.

They got to the hospital fast, and yet it also seemed to take an age. Seb still wasn't responding, but the ECG leads told them he had a good heart rate. That was good. *Something* had to be good in all this.

She was feeling incredibly sick. And guilty. Her son had been dreadfully ill next door, deteriorating, and she'd not known because she'd been sleeping with Jacob!

Eva exhaled heavily and stared at her son. Willing him to read her mind.

Stay strong. I need you, Seb. I need you.

Jacob gripped the steering wheel tightly as the ambulance sped away from him, its lights turning the street blue, then black, in an ever-flickering wail of pain that seared straight to his gut.

What was wrong with Seb? He was no paediatrician— the headache could be anything. But it was the only clue to this whole mess.

Everyone had headaches at some point in their lives— it didn't necessarily mean anything. What did it mean for Seb? He was pale, unconscious. There were a variety of things it could be. An infection…something wrong with his brain. A blood disorder. It could be anything. Something to do with the bang on the head he'd received during that accident on the day he'd found out about his son.

He was a doctor, and all those possibilities were popping into his brain and then out again as he dismissed the thought that it could be any of those things.

He couldn't lose Seb. Not now. He'd only just got to know him. He'd only just begun to appreciate what it was like to have such a wonderful son. To lose him now would be life's cruel trick…

Christmas Eve! It's Christmas Eve again! I'm not going to lose him!

He'd only just found his son… What man wouldn't be thrilled to find out that he had a handsome, strapping young boy? And he was so clever, too—and popular at nursery. Everyone wanted to be Seb's friend. Everyone wanted to sit next to him. He was a good kid. Diligent. They didn't want to know him because he was the class clown. He was a good friend. A nice boy.

The best.

Only now he was lying in the back of an ambulance, speeding to A&E. How had that happened? How had two doctors—two *accident and emergency* doctors—not noticed that their child was ill? Sickening for something?

Had there been earlier signs? Had they missed them?

Jacob cursed.

His stomach roiled with nausea and he rubbed at his forehead as a sharp pain shot across his brow.

The ambulance was way ahead of him now. There was no chance he could keep up. Not safely anyway. He wasn't trained to drive like that, and if he wanted to get to the hospital in one piece himself he knew he had to be patient. Had to be careful.

The traffic lights ahead of him turned red and he cursed them out loud in Afrikaans.

The lights took an age. Or so it seemed. It was probably only twenty seconds or so that he waited, but for Jacob, watching the ambulance disappear in front of him, it was tantamount to torture. His heart was in that ambulance. If he knew anything right now it was that.

His whole life was in that ambulance. Seb. Eva. His future.

What would happen if he lost either one of them? He shook his head, refusing to go down that avenue. It would drive him mad with insanity. He couldn't tolerate the thought—it was just too painful. He felt his heart almost shudder at the thought and bile ran up into his throat.

No. Not that. No. I forbid it.

He couldn't lose them. Not now. He'd only just found them. He'd only just expanded his world to allow them in. And now that he had, his life shone bright. Like a brand-new star in the night sky. He couldn't imagine the future without either one of them.

He'd come back to find Eva. To set things right again. Surely it wasn't all about to go wrong a second time?

The lights turned green and he gunned the engine, shooting forward. He had to remind himself to be careful. He overtook a slow driver and glared at the young man behind the wheel of the car as he passed. Did he not *know* he had to be somewhere? That his son could be *dying*? *Get out of the way!*

Just a mile or two from the hospital now. Not long and he could be back by Seb's side. Standing with Eva to be there for their son. Together. As they always should have been from the start.

He would not be leaving her to fight this fight on her own.

He briefly thought about calling his parents. Then

everyone who loved and cared for Seb could be there at his bedside to support him.

We'll get you through this, Seb. We need you to get through it. I need you to.

There was the exit he needed for the hospital.

Jacob looked out through the windscreen at the bleak landscape. It was all greys and dark browns. The ground was hard and frosted, the trees lifeless and still. He could just see cars and exhaust fumes and frustrated drivers, impatient people hurrying everywhere, trying to get home to their families. To their warm hearths and jolly Christmas jumpers and repeats on the television.

He was frozen in time.

He paused for a moment, pulling over onto the hard shoulder briefly, whilst he fought against nausea and the fear.

He hesitated, took a breath, then pulled back out into the traffic.

CHAPTER EIGHT

THIS WAS SO ALIEN. So strange. To be the one standing back and watching other doctors fuss around her son.

Her son.

This was no random stranger, brought in from the streets. This was no drink-addled unknown blaring out 'Silent Night', or a faltering pensioner with a dodgy ticker. This was *her child*. Her *son*. Her reason for living.

And they were sticking him with needles. Each piercing of his skin pierced her heart, causing her to flinch. She watched him bleed as they searched for venous access and felt her heart breaking into a thousand tiny pieces.

An intravenous drip—a bag of clear fluid—hung by his bedside… Always so innocuous before, but now seeming so threatening. He clearly needed fluids.

How long since he'd last drunk anything? She didn't *know*. She hadn't been with him. She'd been with Jacob!

Machines beeped. Doctors fussed. Vacutainers popped. Voices called out.

'Stat.'

'Do it now!'

She glanced at the readouts on the machines. His pulse was high, his pressure low.

They kept pushing her back. Politely. She was getting

in their way, she knew it, but she *had* to see him. *Had* to keep contact with him. Hold his hand. See his face.

As he lay there she thought back through his whole life. Her pregnancy... Waddling her way through work at the hospital. Those blissful few weeks of maternity leave when she'd been able to put her feet up and rest...

Only she hadn't rested, had she? She'd shopped for baby clothes, for nappies, for equipment—a pushchair, a cot. She'd got the nursery ready, decorating a room for the first time and tipping paint all over her shoes. Then there had been all that palaver with getting the mural on the wall. By the time she'd finished it she'd hated all the characters, only loving them again when she'd taken a step back to marvel at the finished room.

She'd wanted the world perfect for her son. Fatherless, she'd wanted him to have everything else.

The day he was born... Hours and hours of labour, during which she'd been determined to give birth naturally, in her longed-for water birth. The pain had been intense. She'd almost caved and asked for pain relief. She'd always thought she was a tough cookie. But then Seb had been laid in her arms... His chubby arms and legs, his scrunched up fingers and toes and his button nose. His shock of dark hair... He'd looked so much like Jacob she'd almost dropped him.

Almost.

But she'd never let him go. How could she? He'd been perfect. Gazing up at her with eyes so blue she'd thought that the whole world's supply of the colour had gone into his eyes and she would never see a blue thing ever again. Kingfishers would be dull. Bluebells would be just...bells. So blue his eyes had been...

Then there'd been the first time he'd said *mama*. He'd been on the verge of saying it for a long time. Sounding out the *m* for ages, saliva dribbling down his chin as he chomped his lips together over and over, and then... 'Mama.' Heavenly. Perfect. She'd scooped him up and smiled at him so broadly, and he'd smiled back, giggling, and she'd known then, as she knew now, that the perfect little boy she held in her arms would hold all the power over her heart for the rest of her life.

His first attempt at walking—toddling on his chubby legs. Each new day in his short life had given him more and more independence, taking him further and further away from her as he learned what he could do for himself. And still her love for him had grown and grown...

Only he looked lifeless now.

Sleeping, but worse. Pale and unresponsive. Not how he'd ever been and not how a three-year-old should be.

He should be awake, getting excited about Christmas Day tomorrow, sitting in front of the television set or playing outside. Doing a final bit of Christmas shopping with her, perhaps. Helping her make biscuits. Licking out the bowl when she made the icing...

Not here.

Not in a hospital bed with needles and cannulas and IV drips and heart monitors and ventilators and all manner of other things going on.

I can't do this. I can't see him like this.

'He needs a CT.'

She glanced at the doctor and felt alone. *So alone!* Where was Jacob? She *needed* him. Needed him more than she'd ever needed anyone. She shouldn't have to face this alone. Whatever was happening to her son. Whatever the CT might reveal. This wasn't the sort of thing she should do by herself. Hadn't she put herself through hell so she could rely on him? Hadn't she let him in so she could share this responsibility with someone else?

She'd always thought herself strong. Independent. Looking out for herself and Seb in the best way she knew how. And she'd done well at that. But this...? This was something else. This was a torment and a cruelty that she couldn't face alone.

I need you, Jacob!

Eva couldn't tear her eyes away. She needed to see what they were doing to her son. What they *weren't* doing.

They were good doctors. The best. She *knew* these people. It wasn't as if she'd put him into the hands of strangers.

She knew what they suspected.

Words wouldn't soothe. Reassurances didn't matter. Not until your child was whole and well again did anything matter.

Eva felt awful for the way she'd always been so detached with everyone else's kids. But she'd had to be. If she'd got attached, or personally involved, allowed her feelings to interfere, then she'd have been a worn-out wreck.

Only now she was on the other side. Not the doctor. The relative. *She* was the grief-stricken mother. *She* was the one with tears staining her cheeks, her eyes red, searching for hope. *She* was the one grasping at straws and hoping beyond anything that today's doctors and today's medicine could save her child.

Eva felt so alone. So isolated.

But deep down she knew she wasn't. There was Jacob. Somewhere...

Where *was* he? Why wasn't he here yet? Was he still driving to the hospital? Madly searching for a parking bay? Who cared about getting a parking ticket? He should be here by now. Perhaps even now he was running to the A&E department?

Her shoulders went back and her chin came up as grim determination strengthened her.

He's coming. I know he's coming!

She looked at Seb's pale face.

She'd never had to face a crisis like this before. And she felt so lonely.

For the first time in years she wanted her mum.

Jacob blew through the doors of his own A&E department, bypassed Reception and, jacket flying, ran into the maze of corridors that had become like a second home. His gaze flicked to the admissions board but he couldn't see Seb's name.

So he wasn't in cubicles. Nor in Minors.

He had to be in Majors.

Or Resus.

Oh, my God.

He tried to swallow, but his mouth had gone dry. People he worked with tried to say, 'Hi, Merry Christmas!' But he brushed past them and rushed into Resus—where he found Eva by their son's bed. Her eyes were swollen and she held Seb's limp hand in her own.

'Where have you *been*?' she demanded.

Jacob looked shocked. 'I couldn't find a place to park. What's going on? What have they said?'

'They don't know.' She turned back to her son and clasped his hand again. 'They've run tests, done a CT. We're awaiting results.'

'How is he?'

'The same. They want to move him to Paediatric ICU.'

'When?'

She shook her head. 'I don't know. When they can.'

She had no energy for Jacob now that he was here. All her focus was on her boy.

It wasn't good enough. How many times had he impotently stood by, waiting for a bed space to become available? How many times had he had to console a relative because the beds manager couldn't sort out a bed backlog? Too many times. He'd not been working here for long and he was already fed up with the bureaucracy of the hospital and the stupid red tape that stopped them being able to discharge patients who didn't need to be there.

Jacob turned and grabbed the wall phone, almost ripping it from its lodging as he punched in the number for the bed manager.

'Rick?'

'Yes?'

'Dr Dolan in A&E. My son is here in Resus, awaiting a paediatric ICU bed. What's the hold-up?'

There was a pause, during which he heard a brief shuffling of papers. 'Paediatric ICU is full at present. I understand there may be a bed free soon—though I believe there's a possibility that your son may need surgery first.'

'Surgery?'

He saw Eva's face blanch.

'That's not good enough, Rick. My son needs the care of the paediatric team and he needs it *now*. Where's Bilby? Surely he's in today?'

William Bilby was the top paediatric doctor in the entire UK, and he happened to work at their hospital. He'd won awards for the work that he'd carried out in neurological medicine, and families came from across the country to consult him.

'He's not here today. He's on Christmas vacation with his family.'

'Call him.'

'That's not in my remit, Dr Dolan.'

'Then, I'll call him myself!'

There was a sigh. 'Look, I'm sorry about your son being

ill, but we all have to stick to what we do best for the efficient running of this hospital. I can't prioritise your son…'

'Well, I will!'

He slammed the phone back onto the wall, almost crushing it beneath his grip, and turned to look at Eva. She was pale and shocked.

What was he thinking? She needed him to be strong—not for him to turn into some angry monster. He'd lost his temper badly once before and look at how *that* had turned out.

'Sorry,' he mumbled. Then he went across to Seb's bed and took his son's other hand, held it to his cheek. 'Come on, champ…' He looked at Eva, determined not to cry.

Her eyes were large and swollen with tears. 'You said surgery?'

'They must have found something on the CT. Why has no one come to see us?'

He hated this. Hated this not knowing. This being left in limbo.

She shook her head and a solitary tear descended her cheek. 'Am I going to lose him? *Am* I? I don't think I could bear it, Jacob.'

'We're not going to lose him.' He squeezed his son's hand, hoping somehow that the force of his will would somehow make it so.

At that moment, the doors to Resus opened and Sarah came in, her face full of concern. She went straight over to Eva and Jacob. 'We've had a good look at the CT and the scan confirms that Seb has a small subdural haematoma. It's probably been bleeding for a while, as these injuries are usually slow leaks—as you know.'

'You think it's from that bus crash a couple of weeks ago? He banged his head then.'

'It's likely.'

Jacob frowned. 'The neurologist said he didn't need a scan. The *idiot*! He *missed* this!'

'We all missed it, Jacob.' Eva laid a hand on his arm.

Sarah looked to her friend. 'We'll be taking Seb in for surgery right away. Once we get in there we'll clip the leak and remove the haematoma. That should relieve the pressure on Seb's brain.'

'And he'll regain consciousness?'

'Hopefully.'

Hopefully...

Eva shrugged. 'What do we do whilst we wait?'

Sarah just looked at her. 'Try to remain calm. We'll look after him, Eva. You know we'll do our best.'

They could only hope the hospital's best was good enough.

Jacob stood up and began to pace the floor, glaring through the glass at people carrying on with their normal lives whilst his was in turmoil.

Of course they all had jobs to do. He knew that. But he couldn't understand how these other people could be so calm whilst he felt...

He could be losing his family here. His precious family! His *son*! His beloved son! The one he hadn't known he had—the one he'd only just got to know, to love, to cherish. He'd thought a few days before that the worst thing in the world would be to tell Eva the truth about what had happened in his past, but he'd been wrong. You had to tell people you loved them because you never knew when they might be taken from you.

This was what was terrible! This was the worst thing *ever*!

'I'm going to call my parents.'

Eva nodded. 'But they'll be upset. So far away, they won't be able to do anything.'

'They'll want to know.'

She acceded, and then turned back to look at the empty space where her son had been.

Eva had thought she was very familiar with the sensations of pain and grief and loss. She'd also thought she was familiar with waiting. Being patient. But she'd had no clue as to the real agony parents went through whilst they waited to hear if their child had made it through life-saving surgery.

She stared at the doors where the surgeons would emerge, praying, begging, pleading for them to open so that someone would come and tell her that Seb was fine. But the doors stubbornly remained closed. For hours.

When they did finally open—when the surgeon did finally emerge—she almost couldn't bear to hear his words, convinced it had all gone wrong.

The surgeon removed the mask from his face and smiled. 'The surgery went very well. No problems. Seb was stable all the way through. You'll have your little boy back with you in no time.'

Eva sagged with relief at the news. *Thank God!*

The staff in Paediatric ICU had done their best to make it *not* look like a department in a hospital. The walls were painted in a soft cornflower blue, bright and brash with cartoon characters from all kinds of series in a kind of cheery, animated Bayeux Tapestry.

The nurses all wore colourful tabards, with teddy bear name badges edged in tinsel, and there were Christmas trees galore, all surrounded with fake presents—empty boxes wrapped in colourful paper. From the ceilings hung paper chains and the children's snowflakes and snowmen, fat Santas and reindeer.

There was too much effort to make it look jolly.

Fake jolly.

To make the parents as well as the children forget that they were in such a terrible place.

Jacob felt as if he was in hell. The one day he'd hoped would pass without incident and it had turned into the day his nightmares about life came true.

This hurt. He ached. He felt powerless. As both a doctor *and* a father. Now he realised why family was so important. He wanted them here. He wanted their support.

He was glad he'd told Eva the truth.

He still didn't know her reaction. She'd not really had a chance to say. She hadn't looked horrified…but then they'd heard about Seb. She hadn't had a chance to let it sink in.

She might not want anything to do with him. A man who could be so cruel to someone he'd supposedly loved…

If he'd treated Michelle right in the first place—respected her, not taken her for granted once that ring was on her finger—then his happiness now wouldn't be at such great risk!

Eva was the one who had given him Seb. Eva was the one who had cared for and looked after their little boy so well. And then he'd turned up on the day of Seb's accident, distracting her. They'd both been distracted. Both shocked by seeing the other. And they'd missed what had been happening to Seb.

Eva was going to be the one to choose what happened to them all now.

He stared at her, memorising her face. The soft arch of her eyebrows, the laughter lines at her eyes. The gentle slope of her tear-stained cheek. The deep lines across her brow.

'We still need to talk,' he said.

'I can't—not right now.'

He understood. This was the wrong time. She would probably want to wait until Seb was back with them both before she let him down gently.

Hopefully, she would still let him see Seb…

London at dusk was an ethereal place. The sky above was a strange watercolour mix of blue and pink. Purple undertones highlighted the clouds against the dark grey outlines of the buildings. Bright spots of Christmas lights shone out from various streets and windows, and the traffic on the myriad streets below made the place seem alive.

Jacob looked out across the skyline and unclenched his fists. Fear had caused all of this. Fear of losing a boy he'd only just come to love. Fear of losing something, *someone* so precious…

He was calmer now. More sensible now that he knew Seb was going to be okay.

Reaching into his jacket pocket, he pulled out his phone, scrolling through his contacts until he found the number he wanted. William Bilby. The UK's top paediatrician.

It rang a few times, then was answered, the sound fuzzy.

'Hello?'

'Bill? It's Jacob Dolan—'

'No need to say anything, Jacob. I'm on my way in right now. I'm about five minutes from the hospital.'

He was on his way in? But who'd told him about Seb?

'How did you know?'

'Rick told me. He gave me a call. But I've had to drive in from Surrey and the roads are hell.'

Rick. The beds manager. The man he'd yelled at. Jacob closed his eyes in thanks, knowing he would make sure he apologised to the poor man when he got the chance.

'Kids bounce back, Jacob. Much better than adults do.'

'I hope so.'

He rang off, staring out to the horizon. He knew he ought to go back. Knew he shouldn't have left Eva like that. Alone in that horrible empty room. But he'd had to get out. Had to get some fresh air. Be away from other people. The rooftop offered that solace he craved.

His phone bleeped to life.

How's Seb?

His mother had texted. He could only imagine their panic and pain. Could see in his mind's eye his mother's frantic scurrying to get in the car and head from Netherfield Village to London. A place she didn't really like. Today of all days. Leaving her home at Christmastime…

The cold fresh air had done its job, and the chill was now making him tremble and shiver.

And Bilby was coming in, too. He felt sure they could get all this sorted.

Seb had to be out of Recovery soon… Was he already back?

I ought to check. I ought to be there when they bring Seb back to us.

The fresh air had helped. The space. The crispness.

He headed back down.

As Seb was wheeled back into the room a new doctor arrived. Mr Bilby. Eva wasn't sure, but she thought this was the man that Jacob had asked for when he'd rung the beds manager. Whoever he was, he had a kind face with a wide smile, and he did his best to put Eva at her ease.

'I've read the report. The surgery was a great success. We've got Seb's back here—don't you worry.'

Good. He knew they were doing their best.

They all rushed over to Seb's side when his bed wheels had been locked into position.

Jacob grabbed his son's hand and kissed it, then turned around, nodding an acknowledgement of Mr Bilby. 'Bill.'

'Observations are good, Jacob. He should come round soon.'

'Good.'

'Temp's normal. BP's normal. We've just got to wait for the sedation to wear off.'

William Bilby slipped away and left them alone together. Silent beside their son's bed.

Jacob stared into space, his face shockingly white against his dark hair, his once vibrant blue eyes pale and cold.

Eva stood numb beside him as they both stared at their son. Each of them praying in their own special way.

Early on Christmas Day Seb slowly woke up.

Eva woke instantly, as if by some sixth sense, and heard Jacob say his son's name.

She leaped to her feet, blinking rapidly to get the sleep from her eyes so she could see for herself the marvellous result of her son coming back to her.

'Seb? Sebastian? Oh, thank God! You're back!'

Seb blinked slowly, his eyes unfocused, but he gently gripped his mother's fingers and then closed his eyes again.

'He'll be tired. He might sleep more before he wakes again,' Jacob observed.

Eva glanced at him. 'I'm scared to think that this might end well. I've hoped that way before.'

'His observations are good. His intercranial pressure is normal. We *can* hope, Eva.'

She stroked her son's fringe back from his face. 'You wanted to talk earlier?'

He looked up at her and met her gaze, his heart palpitating in his chest. Of course. He'd promised himself—promised them all—that he would face this. Her judgement of his actions.

It was the only way he could set himself free. If she chose to walk, then so be it. He wouldn't blame her. But he *had* to know he would still have Seb! He couldn't lose him.

I don't want to lose her, either. I love her!

He swallowed and looked back at his sleeping son. He didn't want them to break up in front of their son. He believed that Seb might hear them. He wanted this to be private. He wanted the opportunity to talk to her without any chance of interruptions.

'I know where we can talk.'

Giving one final look of love at Seb, he led Eva outside and up onto the hospital roof.

CHAPTER NINE

EVA BEGAN TO SHIVER. And it wasn't just from the cold. 'What is it?'

'It's Michelle.'

Michelle. I knew it! He still carries a torch for her! He still loves her!

'What about her?'

She needed to hear him say it. If he still loved this woman from his past, then fine. She would walk away. She would do the decent thing. Because if the past twenty-four hours had taught her anything, it was that the most important thing in her life was Seb.

'It's *my* fault she's dead. *I* killed her, Eva.'

Eva looked at him, incredulous. 'No, you didn't!'

'Of course I did. Didn't you hear what I said? I didn't treat her right. I got complacent, got stupid. I should have seen what was going on! But I didn't. And because I didn't, I yelled at her. As if it was *her* fault! I upset her so much she couldn't see where she was going and she crashed.'

'I heard you, Jacob. It was terrible, I grant you—tragic—but you weren't to blame.'

He'd been expecting to hear her agree with him. To start blaming him, too. But she didn't. The shock of hearing something else startled him.

'I wasn't?'

'*No!* She chose to have an affair, Jacob. She could have told you how she was feeling—but, no, she cheated on you with your best friend! And, whilst we're at it, *he* should have known better, too! No one forced her into her car that day. She was upset—she should never have driven. She has to take responsibility.'

'I feel so guilty…'

'Of course you do. You're human. *I'd* feel guilty. But don't forget everyone else on that day and how they must have felt.'

'What do you mean?'

'The driver of the heavy-goods vehicle. Do you think *he* felt guilty? Do you think the paramedics felt guilty because they couldn't revive her? The doctors in the hospital? We both work in A&E—you know how we feel when we lose someone.'

Jacob stared at her hard, his eyes glassy with held-back tears. 'I was so afraid of telling you… I thought I would lose you.'

Eva shivered slightly in the cold. 'What? You thought I'd say it was over? You think you're not worth staying for?'

'I've caused so much pain, Eva.'

'The only thing that will cause more will be if you tell me that you still love her!'

Jacob looked at her in shock. As if it was the last thing he'd be feeling. 'I don't love her.' He looked confused by her statement. 'I never loved her *enough.*'

What? What was he saying? Eva didn't understand.

'I don't understand. Are you in love with her or not?'

'No. I love *you.*' He looked down at the pitched felt rooftop. 'You deserved the truth from me. But if you want to walk away from me now you know it…I'll understand.'

'Walk away? Don't you *get* it, Jacob? I *need* you! I never thought I'd be able to say that about anyone. *Ever!* Apart from Seb…but he's part of me… I knew I loved you ages ago. But I felt I couldn't tell you because I thought you still loved Michelle and that hurt! As I stood by Seb's bed, watching the doctors work, watching them trying to fix him, I felt so alone! And I'm done with that feeling. I'm *done*! You and I… We're… We could have something really special. I knew it all those years ago, when we first met. There was something special between us then.'

'What are you saying, Eva?'

'I'm saying I want to be with you. Together. As a family.'

'But what happened to Michelle—'

'Was a tragic accident! Nothing more! I need you to let that go.'

Jacob sucked in a breath. 'Without you and Seb I'm nothing. I can't let *you* go.'

She stepped closer, pulling the warmth of him against her. 'You don't have to.'

'You mean it?' He hesitantly risked a smile.

'I mean it.'

She reached up on tiptoes and kissed him, and she forgot how cold she was, pressed against him. Feeling herself against him.

With him.

'I spent so long standing alone, Jacob. It was just easier for me, I thought, to push you away before you left of your own accord. I thought I was protecting myself. Protecting my heart from being crushed.'

'I'll never hurt your heart. I'll always cherish it. I'll always cherish *you*.'

She reached up and stroked his face, and as she did so snowflakes began to fall. A soft flurry of snow, sweeping in across the capital in the morning light.

They looked about them in wonder, and then back at each other.

'It's snowing! On Christmas Day! Seb will love this!'

Eva snuggled into his chest, feeling safe, feeling *home*.

'So we're going to do this? Together?'

She nodded. 'Together.'

They kissed.

As the snow fell all around them on the rooftop of the hospital, alone in their own special little world they kissed. Their cold noses pressed against the cheek of the other, and their hot breath warmed their mouths and lips as they proved their commitment to the other.

When they broke apart Jacob looked her in the eyes. 'I love you, Eva. From the moment we met I haven't been able to get you out of my head. You've always been there for me. Even in the dark times. Even when you didn't know it.'

Eva let out a big grin. He loved her!

'I love you, too, Jacob.'

'You do?'

She nodded, then shivered. 'But could we go back inside? I hate to be the one to spoil a romantic moment, but I'm freezing!'

Jacob wrapped his arm around her as they hurried back to the rooftop door. There was a bang in the stairwell as it closed behind them, and they ran down the steps, laughing and breathing heavily.

Back in Seb's room, they found he was still sleeping, so they sat beside each other, knowing Seb would get better, that this story would have a happy ending for all of them. And soon, hopefully, Seb would be out and about on his new bike.

Jacob raised her hand to his lips and kissed it.

When Seb woke again he would have the best Christmas present he could ever have wished for.

EPILOGUE

'I'D LIKE TO make a toast!'

Jacob stood in the lounge of his parents' home, in front of the vast fireplace. A small fire was crackling away, keeping them all warm and cosy despite the fresh snowfall outside.

A whole year had passed, and this Christmas Eve had thankfully arrived without incident.

Eva and Jacob had been married for three months. Their September wedding had gone without a hitch, despite his nerves about it being to the contrary, and this last year had been the happiest of their lives.

He raised his glass to his family, looking at all their happy, smiling faces. There were still one or two pieces of Christmas wrapping paper on the carpet that had been missed, but that didn't matter. Seb was sitting on the carpet, surrounded by a big pile of toys and wearing the paper hat from a Christmas cracker. Eva sat between his parents on the couch, feeling very full after his mother's most ambitious Christmas yet.

'I'd like to raise a toast to family,' he said, raising his glass once again before letting his gaze come to rest on Eva. 'Family is the heart of everything. You don't have to be blood relatives to be family. You just need to be surrounded by those you love and those who love you back. Love is the greatest thing we can give one other.'

Eva beamed at him and gave a little nod.

'But most of all I'd like to make a toast to my wife, Eva…'

His parents raised their glasses and looked towards her.

Eva felt excited. Nervous. She'd been dreaming about this moment for a long time. About telling them. Seeing how they reacted. Because this time she was going to share the experience. This time, she wouldn't be going through anything alone.

'And to the baby she's carrying.'

Molly almost dropped her glass. She gasped, her hand covering her mouth in genuine surprise and joy. 'You're *pregnant*?'

Eva nodded happily.

'You're pregnant! Oh, Eva!' Molly burst into tears and hugged her daughter-in-law, and Eva hugged her back.

This was what she'd wanted. For a long time.

Family.

To belong.

To be loved.

'To family!' she said.

They all raised their glasses, and they were just about to clink them together before taking a sip when Molly grinned and swiped Eva's champagne flute, swapping it for her own—non-alcoholic—orange juice.

'To *family*.'

* * * * *

MILLS & BOON®

Christmas Collection!

Unwind with a festive romance this Christmas
with our breathtakingly passionate heroes.
Order all books today and receive a free gift!

Order yours at
www.millsandboon.co.uk
/christmas2015

1015_MB515

MILLS & BOON®

Buy A Regency Collection today
and receive FOUR BOOKS FREE!

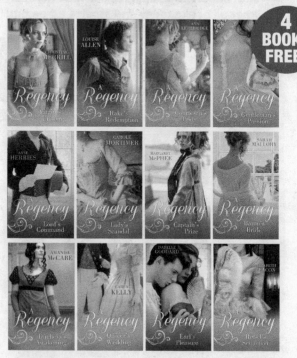

Transport yourself to the seductive world of Regency
with this magnificent twelve-book collection.
Indulge in scandal and gossip with these
2-in-1 romances from top Historical authors

Order your complete collection today at
www.millsandboon.co.uk/regencycollection

MILLS & BOON®

MEDICAL ROMANCE™

THE ULTIMATE IN ROMANTIC MEDICAL DRAMA

15/03